Off Limits

A Brother's Best Friend Steamy Romance

Emma Jay

Chapter One

Zach Purser stood at the edge of the dance floor and watched the woman in the cream-colored dress move to the music, hips swaying, arms twisting sinuously over her head. A cascade of reddish-brown curls tumbled around her shoulders, hair he would love to bury his face in while he cupped her hips and drew her back against him. He'd always been an ass man.

His best friend Adam Clark joined him at the rail overlooking the dance floor. "Surprised you haven't hit on anyone already. Or that someone hasn't hit on you."

Zach's lips twisted. "I have my eye on one."

"The blonde? Because she's married."

Right. Adam knew more of the people here than he did, since this was his brother Matt's engagement party to J.R., the man he'd been dating for years. Something to celebrate, no doubt. Zach could respect their joy, the difficulties they'd overcome. Zach tended to avoid any difficulties if he could help it.

"Not the blonde, though, damn." Great tits, and Zach had already pictured her naked and riding him.

"The little brunette? She's a sweetheart but too young for you."

"How young?" Zach scoped out the slender girl in the tight black dress, just in case.

"Twenty, I think. Maybe twenty-one."

Definitely too young, too many romantic ideas. "No. The one with the great ass and the great hair."

Adam chuckled. "Which one's that?"

"The curls, the white dress."

The chuckle died and Adam straightened. "You haven't seen her face."

Zach frowned. How did Adam know that? "No, but—"

Adam punched his arm, hard. "That's my sister, asshole. Don't even think about going near her. I know your MO. Got it?"

Just then, the object of his fantasy turned, still moving to the music, and he looked into the heart-shaped face of Paige Clark, who he'd known since he was in high school and she was in, what, fourth grade? He should feel dirty, lusting after his best friend's sister, for the fantasies he'd already had about her. But damn, she'd grown up nice, that gorgeous hair he could already feel beneath his fingers, full breasts—ah, God—and those hips.

Adam punched his arm again, harder. "Quit thinking about it. Christ. She's too good for you."

No doubt. But yeah, Adam was right. Living out that fantasy would be beyond weird. Not like there weren't other women, available and willing. But his attention was drawn to Paige, her sexy movements, her beautiful smile, and Jesus, that body.

She lifted her gaze and met his. He took a step back at the sultry curve of her mouth. Did she recognize him? Because, damn, that was the smile of a woman who wanted to get laid.

His best friend's baby sister.

He braced his hands against the rail, then spun away. "Right. You know, maybe I'd better head out."

Adam's smile was tight. "No self-control?"

"Not really one to celebrate commitments, no matter what form."

Adam shook his head. "And you wonder why I want you away from my sister."

"Okay, so I'll catch up with you later." He turned and made his way through the crowd with a wave at Matt and J.R., edging past eligible women who just didn't do it for him, not tonight.

"Hey, where you going?" A slender hand on his arm stopped Zach on his way out the door.

He looked down into the sloe eyes of Paige Clark. He commanded his attention to stay on her face, though had she always had that full mouth that he could imagine fulfilling his fantasies? And just on the edge of his vision, he could see the swell of her breasts. Time to go. Adam's sister. His best friend for half his life.

"I can't believe you were going to leave without saying hello."

He turned to face her, forcing himself to be friendly, but keeping his guard up. He was unaccustomed to watching himself around women—the more outrageous he was, the more they liked it.

"Hello, Rage."

She laughed, delighted at his teasing tone. "You would remember that."

"You had more temper tantrums than anyone I knew before or since."

"But now I'm all grown up." She swept her hands down her sides.

At least he thought she did because he focused on her face.

But not on her mouth. Too many wicked images came with that view. "You're very lovely."

"You look the same." Something playful lurked beneath the smile that he wasn't looking at.

"How long has it been? Five years?"

She cocked her hip, tilting her head so her hair tumbled over one shoulder. "Seven. I'm twenty-four now, graduated and working as a shopper, if you can believe it."

He frowned. "You used to hate shopping." That he remembered that about her surprised him.

"Because I couldn't find anything that fit me."

"You were a scrawny little thing."

"I filled out." Those sloe eyes dared him to see for himself.

He resisted. Barely. But the image of her moving on the dance floor was etched into his brain.

She tucked her hand in his. "Come dance with me."

Not a good idea. He'd be touching her, at the very least watching her. Already he was doing everything in his power to stop his arousal. Those skills were rusty, because he always gave in. The reason Adam wanted him far away from Paige. "I need to go."

"One dance." She tugged his hand, and he took a step toward the dance floor, resisting the urge to search the room for Adam. She gave him a look that said she wasn't taking no for an answer.

He could manage a short time in her arms, then never see her again. Who knew where they would be in another seven years? He squared his shoulders and nodded. She wriggled in delight and turned to haul him close, his hand tucked in the small of her back. Right above that gorgeous ass.

Once she'd found the spot she wanted, she turned to him, moving with such sensual grace that for a moment he froze in place. He was a good dancer—at least he'd been told—but for the life of him, he couldn't make his body move as he watched her, the sway of her hair, the undulation of her spine, every movement making his imagination work overtime. She laughed and pushed at his chest, as if that would jumpstart him.

She turned her back on him, and that did the trick. Without thinking, he gripped her hips and drew her against him, moving into her. She shivered and looped her arms behind his neck.

Too late he realized his mistake. A hand gripped his shoulder and spun him around. He barely registered the cold anger on Adam's face before the fist crashed into his eye.

Zach crossed the room to answer the doorbell and squinted through the peephole. No way. He debated opening the door, but his fingers had already made the decision, unhooking the safety latch. Yeah, the story of his life, his body making decisions before his brain could think it through.

He swung the door open and faced Paige, who stood in the hall, hands on her hips, her shapely body clad in low-riding jeans and a snug T-shirt. Her lips pursed in concern as she stepped through the door and touched his temple. He winced and ducked before she could touch the bruised flesh around his eye.

"I am so sorry."

"He warned me to keep my hands off of you. I should have listened."

"He's being overprotective."

"Rightly so. He knows me better than you do."

That pretty mouth twisted as she inspected his bruise. "Did you put ice on it? Thank goodness you didn't need stitches."

It had bled plenty, but was only a small cut. "Chicks dig scars. And I had an ice pack in the freezer."

"It still looks swollen to me." She pushed past him into the apartment and hesitated before reasoning out where the kitchen was. "Have a seat."

He heard the opening and closing of the freezer and followed her into the kitchen. He needed to get rid of her. If Adam knew she'd come over...

"How do you know where I live?"

She gave the ice pack a whack against the counter to loosen it up. "You're easy enough to find. Now sit." She motioned to the chair at the table.

Better here than in the living room, and if he obeyed, maybe she'd leave before he found himself in trouble. She pressed the pack to his temple, curving her hand around his cheek. The pack might be better placed on his crotch as he struggled not to look at the way the soft knit of her T-shirt gapped just a bit when she bent over.

"Maybe the question should be, why did you find me?"

"Because I felt terrible about Adam punching you. It's my fault."

"My fault." He stretched his legs out in front of him with the intention of pushing her away. Okay, that wasn't very comfortable. He folded them under the chair and wished for something to drop over his lap. "He gave me fair warning."

"But I didn't give you a choice." She crouched beside him, her face angled up to him.

Not better. His cock twitched at a wicked image that popped into his mind. "There's another chair over there."

"I know."

"Paige, you shouldn't be here."

"Why? Are you the big bad wolf?" She leaned forward and rested her palm on his chest, no doubt feeling the uptick of his heartbeat at her nearness.

"Very nearly. I thought Adam would have told you as much."

"He told me you were no good for me. I think that's a fine way to talk about his friend."

"He's right."

"He's not." She shifted between his bent knees and tossed her wild curls over her shoulder.

He tried to pull his knees together, to push her away, but she placed her hand on his stomach, right above his fly. His cock refused to listen to reason—girl on knees, hand near fly—all bets were off. Even if she was his best friend's sister.

"You should go."

"You don't really want me to." She eased forward, edging his thighs farther apart. "I've wanted to do this for so long, Zach, and when I saw you there at the party, looking good enough to eat, when I saw the way you were looking at me, finally, I knew I couldn't let the opportunity pass."

His very last ounce of will allowed him to sit forward in his chair and grip her arms—soft, silky arms, damn it—and look into her eyes. "He's my best friend. I can't."

"You can." She trailed her finger down to tap on the top button of his jeans. "You want to so bad I can taste it." She rolled the word "taste" around in her mouth, and he squeezed his eyes shut against the fresh surge of lust. "And what Adam doesn't know won't hurt him."

"I'll know." So this is why he was never noble. It was damned hard. "Paige. You need to go."

Her smile was downright evil and made him harder than he'd thought possible. "No." She unbuttoned the top button and nudged up the hem of his T-shirt just enough to trail a fingernail over the line of hair leading from his navel to the waistband of his boxer briefs. He couldn't hold back the moan.

"My best friend," he choked.

"I've wanted you to make love to me since I was fourteen years old, since I knew what it could feel like."

Curiosity tugged at him. "How did you know what it could feel like?"

"Do you remember Chris Danvers?"

Anger rolled through him. He did indeed remember the little twit. "He touched you?"

"He kissed me until I was crazy. I figured the rest out for myself."

The image of her touching herself made his mouth dry, and he dropped his head back, rubbing his hand over his good eye.

"You're thinking about it, aren't you?" Her fingers slid under his T-shirt, traced his navel. "You want me to show you?"

Yes. "No." He captured her slender wrist before she could do more damage. With a mental groan, he scooted his chair back and stood, not releasing her wrist. "Sorry, Paige. You need to go."

Wow. She had the puppy-dog eyes down. She withdrew from his grasp with a twist of her wrist. "You're sure?"

"Sure."

"Okay, then." She leaned over the counter and scribbled something on the pad by his phone. "My number if you change your mind."

"I won't."

She swayed that gorgeous ass on the way to the hall, giving him all the time in the world to change his mind. He wouldn't even let his thoughts go there.

But once she was out the door, he was down the hall to the bathroom to jack off, the image of her pretty mouth burned into his mind.

Masturbation didn't stop the desire that pulsed through his blood. He didn't go out that night, but did the next. Despite the club being packed to the rafters with beautiful women, not one was Paige. He'd thrown away her phone number to remove all traces of temptation, but none of the women he watched, none he danced with, aroused the same passion in him.

He got it—the lure of the forbidden. One of his favorite

things. How often had he indulged in an act just because it was taboo? But none of his prior actions would have the implications of bringing Paige to his bed. God, he wanted to bring Paige to his bed.

And Adam would kill him dead.

"What the hell is wrong with you?" Adam demanded when, for the fourth night in a row, Zach walked out of a club with no female companionship.

"Not feeling it."

Adam stared. "Have you ever gone this long without sex?"

"Let it go, Adam." He did not want his friend delving deeper, finding the real reason for his lack of interest. He just wanted to go home, jack off and hopefully clear his mind of Paige and this spell she'd put on him.

It didn't really count that he imagined Paige's mouth on his cock when he came, right?

Adam's phone rang as they walked to the car, and he fished it out of his front pocket.

"Paige," he muttered, and answered, unaware Zach's body had gone on full alert.

Zach tried not to listen, but caught the "Where are you?" part of the conversation before Adam ended the call.

"Paige needs a ride home. You mind?"

"Where is she?" Zach asked, instead of, "Why can't she get a cab?" which would have been wiser.

Adam told him the name of a club, not far away.

"So is she living here in Austin now?" Zach asked as he guided the car out of the parking lot.

"She's been living in the city awhile. Just now making enough money to go out with her friends and have fun. Sounds like one of her friends got lucky and left Paige on her own."

Zach wanted to ask Adam if he realized Paige was looking to get lucky too, and stopped himself from wondering if she had, since their last encounter. He hadn't been able to find another to interest him, but for all he knew, she'd slept with a different guy every night, or worse, found her true love.

She was waiting at the curb outside the club when Zach pulled alongside in his Audi, wearing fuck-me heels and a skirt so short he'd be able to see her panties if she bent—or sat. His own shorts tightened as he did his best not to imagine what delicate garment she might be wearing. He kept his gaze straight ahead as she opened the back door of his car and slid in, buckling in the seat belt before she said, "Thanks, guys. Hi, Zach."

"Hey. Where to?"

"Where were you guys going?"

Zach had been ready to call it a night but hadn't discussed it with Adam, who glanced over. "We were heading out for coffee."

"So early?" Disappointment laced her tone.

"We're old," Zach said.

"Not that old. Not even thirty."

"You say that number like it's a bad word."

She unbuckled and leaned between their seats. "Let's go to another club."

Adam shook his head before Zach could protest. "I'm not going to watch my sister try to pick up some guy, and I sure as hell don't want her there when I'm trying to pick up someone."

"Stick in the mud. Just for a drink, okay?"

Adam hesitated. "One drink. Then we'll take you home."

She sat back, and Zach gave in to the urge to look in the rearview mirror. Just as he expected—her expression one of the cat who ate the cream. She was getting what she wanted, and he would be in misery for the rest of the evening.

Paige's pulse thrummed as she sat across from Zach in the club they'd chosen—a place way tamer than the one she'd just left, with a more sedate, older crowd. She watched Zach lift the highball glass of Scotch to his lips, watched his throat work as he swallowed, and wanted to reach out to touch his skin.

She'd had a crush on him for as long as she could remember, from fourth grade, when he first started hanging around Adam, to high school, when those shoulders had started to fill out, to now, when he was every inch a successful ad executive, with his expensive haircut, his fashionably unshaven jaw, his well-made suit.

He was looking everywhere but at her. Of course, Adam was there, and Adam had punched him in the face for dancing with her. At least that bruise had faded. She took a sip of her martini and pretended not to be uncomfortable as no one at the table spoke.

She knew she looked good. Cristina hadn't been the only one with offers to go home tonight, but Paige only wanted one man. She wanted him to see her, damn it. She slipped out of her chair and bent over to collect her clutch from the floor, giving him an excellent view of her ass as her skirt rode up. He saw, because she heard him choke on his Scotch.

"I'm going to the ladies'. Be right back." Confident that he was watching, she swayed off.

But she was never going to get him to give in as long as Adam was around.

She watched the table for a bit before she returned. No women made a move, which was interesting, but this wasn't exactly a hook-up place. And the two men together, both handsome and well dressed, were pretty intimidating.

Paige approached from behind, out of their line of sight.

"Small of the back," Adam said.

Zach set his glass down on the table with a clink. "You always say that."

"That's where I always hope they are. Why? Where do you think it is?"

"Her hip, right above her panties. Perfect place. A butterfly."

Adam made a sound of derision. "A rose."

Tattoos. She scanned the room. Who were they speculating about? The blonde, maybe, in the pale yellow suit. Or the waitress with the close-cropped red hair and bored expression. That one—the tawny-haired goddess in the jeans and patterned T-shirt.

"Chinese symbol for harmony, right shoulder," Paige added, sliding into her chair.

Both men pivoted toward her and stared. Good. She'd finally gotten Zach to look at her.

"What? You think girls don't play that game? Do you actually get them to show you the tattoos?" She looked from one to the other.

Adam stared at his drink, and she could have sworn she saw a blush creep up his throat. She leaned closer.

"If I ask really nice, they show me theirs. I've seen some tattoos in interesting places." She chanced a glance at Zach and saw a muscle in his jaw twitch. "Did you know guys can get tattoos on their—"

"That's enough." Adam pushed his glass away and rose. "Time to go. No fun drinking with one's sister."

"Oh, I can be fun. Want to watch?"

"No." He hooked his hand around her upper arm. "You need to go home where you're safe."

She thrust her lower lip out in an exaggerated pout. "It's no fun drinking with one's brother. Am I right?" She turned to Zach for back up.

"I like drinking with him. You, on the other hand, make me nervous." He bounced his keys in his palm. "Let's go."

She made him nervous. That was definite progress.

Zach laced his fingers behind his head and stared at the

circling ceiling fan, naked on his bed, hard and aching because of goddamned Paige Clark. He'd masturbated once tonight, but his hand was no substitute for those luscious lips or her sweet pussy, which he almost glimpsed twice earlier when she bent over in that skirt-from-the-devil. What the hell was he supposed to do? He couldn't fuck her because he valued Adam's friendship too much. He was going to have to find a substitute, no question about it. He hadn't exactly had this problem before, had never been so focused on one woman, but he could deal with it.

He gripped his cock and began to stroke.

Chapter Two

This was his element. Zach sat back in the leather chair and watched the two girls on the long couch, the blonde straddling the face of the redhead, who lapped at her slit while the blonde tucked her hair over her ear and covered the redhead's pussy with her open mouth. His cock thrummed, just this side of painful.

He hadn't been to the sex club in months, but it was providing just the distraction he needed. If he wanted, he could get in on this action, or he could crook his finger at the woman at the bar who was watching at a distance and take her back to one of the private rooms, or hell, even approach the couple groping each other at the table by the wall and see if they wanted to try a ménage.

Before he turned back to the two girls, where the redhead was groaning against the blonde's cunt, on the verge of coming, she walked in. He was on his feet before he knew it, not trusting his eyes. Why the hell would Paige Clark be at a sex club? But it was her, those wild curls unmistakable as she giggled with her two friends. He took two strides toward her and stopped. Did he want her to know he visited this establishment? Or was it better to pretend he wasn't here and watch her fuck some random stranger?

Right. Best she knew what he was. He crossed the room and stopped in front of her, blocking her view of the couple he'd considered joining, the woman on the table with her legs spread for her partner's mouth.

"What the hell are you doing here?" he demanded.

Paige angled her head up, those tilted eyes knowing, as if she'd expected him to be here. "Same thing as you."

"No. You're not. Out." He pointed toward the door, shifting whenever her gaze moved past him.

Her friends snickered but he didn't spare them a glance.

"I paid my money. I want to see."

"There's nothing you want to see. This isn't the place for you."

Her eyes snapped back to him and narrowed. "But it's fine for you."

"That I'm a pervert is common knowledge, and the main reason your brother hit me in the face. No telling what he'd do if he knew you were in here."

"I'm a grown-up. I know what I want." She closed the space between them and pressed her hips against his, her lips parting when his erection bumped her belly. She looked in the direction from which he'd come, where the two girls now sat up, sated, and reached for their clothing. "Is that what you like? Two girls? Three-ways?" She rubbed her belly along the length of his cock. "Am I just not enough for you, Zach? Is that why you're pushing me away?"

He gripped her arms, but he couldn't make himself put distance between them. God, her body felt so good. His blood hummed in his veins, the pitch deepening with each bump of her hips. He wanted to pin her to the wall and grind against her, wanted to bury his face in her hair and breathe in her scent.

"You want me." Her breath gusted against his throat. Her breasts brushed his chest, her nipples hard through the thin fabric of her dress.

Which made him wonder if she wore any underwear at all. His gaze dropped to the short skirt. All he had to do was lift it up—

He thought about the private rooms that circled the club, ones with two-way mirrors that allowed the occupants to look out onto the club while they indulged their own desires. He thought about securing one and fucking Paige until she screamed.

Only he didn't want to take her here, didn't want the stain of this place, as extravagant as it was, on her.

"Let's go." He motioned to the door, unwilling to admit aloud that she'd won. But he was taking her to the hotel across the street and screwing her until they were both drained. At least that was more respectable than taking her in the club.

She tossed her hair over her shoulder. "I want a drink first."

He glanced toward the bar, where a guy was giving another guy a blowjob. Paige's eyes widened, her lips parted and she flushed. "I'll buy you a drink somewhere else. The drinks here are watered down anyway."

"I want to watch. You like that, right? Watching? Or were you getting ready to join in?"

A moment passed before he realized she meant join the girls, not the men.

"Do you do it out here?" Her voice was breathy as she moved toward the bar, taking in the couple at the table, the girls stripping each other on the stage, the piped-in cries and moans over the loudspeakers.

He wished the heat flooding his face was because of the alcohol, but he was pretty sure he was embarrassed. That was new. He wanted to convince her to leave. He swallowed. "Sometimes."

She wasn't deterred by his reticence. "Do you bring someone, or meet them here?"

"Usually meet them here."

"Girls, right?" She slanted an uncertain look in his direction.

He needed to get her off the subject and out of this place, but she was determined. "Right. What do you want, a martini?"

She nodded, her back to the bar as she took in the place, the leather and cherry furnishings, expensive carpeting, the Tiffany-style lighting, all bringing to mind an old-fashioned bordello.

"You're blushing," he said as he presented the drink to her. "That kind of gives you away."

"You turned red earlier. I'm thinking you're not as hard as you think you are."

He eased closer. "I'm plenty hard. You, on the other hand, are innocent, and it shows."

She turned to him, her palm on his chest, her thigh riding up his. "What about this? What does this say?"

"It says you'd better say something nice about me at my funeral when Adam kills me." He pinned her to the bar, his hands on either side of the padded cherry wood, and bent to kiss her.

The kiss was everything Paige had imagined it would be, his mouth warm and smooth, the bristle of his stubble teasing the edges of her lips. His tongue swept into her mouth, stroking as his body moved against hers, rubbing against her enough to push up the short hem of her skirt, and—

"Oh!"

He lifted his head, blue eyes dark, lips parted as if he wanted to devour her. "What?"

She tightened her fingers on his sleeves and forced herself to meet his gaze. "I'm close."

His head snapped back and his brows furrowed. "To coming?"

She nodded, trying not to push her pussy against his leg, wanting her first orgasm with him to be, well, with him.

"Christ." He moved away from her as if she was on fire. He pulled out his wallet, tossed a bill on the counter and took her hand.

"Where are we going?" she asked as she stumbled after him and—oh. Wow, she was really turned on. This had never happened before. But then, she'd never walked around in a sex club without underwear, hoping to seduce the lust of her life. Every step was a caress on her swollen clit.

"I kissed you in a sex club. I'm not going to make you come in one."

"Isn't that, like, the point?"

He scowled, barely giving her time to take leave of her friends before he pulled her out the door and onto the sidewalk. He hesitated, as if debating with himself, then charged across the street, pulling her in his wake.

She looked up to see a hotel looming nearby, and not a cheap hotel. This was where he was taking her. This was where he'd make love to her for the first time. A giddiness rose in her as he pulled her through the big glass doors.

"Go wait over there." He pointed to plush, well-appointed chairs in the lobby.

She did as she was told and he walked to the desk. She watched him draw out a credit card and snap it on the desk, saw the clerk glance past him to her. The woman probably saw a lot of similar situations, being this close to a sex club.

Paige still couldn't believe she'd had the courage to walk into that place. She was no virgin, but she'd never played these kinds of games. Maybe it had been a little stalkerish to find out where he was and go after him, but she had learned the only way to get what you wanted was to be bold.

Paige adjusted her skirt before sitting. God, she was so wet she could feel her juices on her thighs, could smell herself. She resisted the urge to rub her legs together, but if there'd been fewer people in the lobby, she might have parted her legs for him when he approached, just to see his reaction.

He said nothing, just held out a hand. She took it, savoring the warmth of his touch, and he led her to the elevator. She followed eagerly, anticipating more kissing and rubbing, though she didn't want to come yet. She wanted him to be fully focused on her when that happened. Once in the elevator car, he stayed on one side and she stayed on the other. Disappointment bloomed in her chest. Did he want her or not? His hands were folded in front of him, his gaze on the changing numbers. She thought about asking what floor their room was on, if the clerk had said anything about them checking in without luggage, if he wanted to split the price of the room, but she didn't want to give him a reason to press the lobby button and send her on her way.

He twitched a little when the door opened with a bing, and motioned for her to exit to the right.

"Use your words, Zach," she prodded, exasperated. She was in no mood to play charades.

"Room seven-forty-two."

She scanned the room numbers then turned to the right, leading the way, pulse drumming. This was going to happen. He was going to make her come, he was going to put his mouth on her, slide inside her. Finally. He slipped past her to open the door, still not speaking, still not looking at her. She waited for him to grab her and slam her against the wall once they were in the room, but he walked past her to the bed, tossing the key card down on the dresser with a slap, like he was mad.

She stood near the door, having no idea what to do now. He was across the room and that suddenly felt like miles.

He dragged his fingers through his hair as he looked at her reflection in the glass of the window. "If I touch you right now, I'll hurt you."

"Then perhaps I should tie you up."

She said it playfully, but he whipped around, his nostrils flared and his eyes dark. Oh, so he liked that idea. Heart pounding, she glanced around the room, searching for what she could use, resting on the front of his shirt. He clapped a hand over it before she could say anything.

"Do you know how much this thing cost?" His gaze floated down the length of her body. "Your panties."

"Not wearing any." Though she suspected he'd known that and just wanted her to say it.

"I wondered. I can smell you." He passed his palm over his face and she could see it was shaking. Good. So was she. "Paige."

"Your belt," she decided, frightened by the way he said her name, that he was going to send her away.

His fingers rested on it a moment, then he unbuckled it quickly, whipped it from the loops and held it out to her.

She moved two steps forward and took it without touching him. The expensive leather was supple under her fingers. She looked from the belt to the bed, the slatted headboard that would be perfect. Zach shrugged out of his jacket and stretched on the bed, his long elegant fingers curling through the slats.

This wasn't exactly how she'd imagined their first time. She'd rather have him touching her, stroking her skin, kissing her mouth. But if this was what he wanted, she'd play along.

"I've never tied anyone up before," she admitted.

"Good," he said, the word rumbling in his throat.

She approached from the other side of the bed and looped

the belt through the slats, then around his wrists as his breathing increased. His legs moved restlessly, his arms tensed as she bent over him. His hot breath gusted against her breasts above the bodice of her dress, and she felt his gaze burning into her. She would not let him scare her away. She looped the leather together, unable to fasten it, and straightened to see her handiwork.

The fine fabric of his white button-down shirt was twisted around his body. She hadn't seen this new Zach disheveled, and that weakness gave her hope. The expensive fabric of his pants tented with his erection she ached to feel. His fingers flexed above the leather, his eyes slitted.

"You're taking your time."

"Payback for you making me wait." She knelt on the bed beside him, her gaze returning to that lovely erection. She made her decision and straddled him, the insides of her thighs against the soft fabric of his slacks. She let her bare pussy brush the placket over his zipper as she reached for the buttons of his shirt.

"Paige!" His voice was strangled, on the barest leash.

She smiled and leaned over to kiss him, her mouth teasing, drawing back when he lifted his tongue to play. How long had she wanted to kiss him, to feel just his mouth and hands arousing her? Later, she promised herself, and sat up to open his shirt. She released the buttons slowly, spreading the fabric as she went, letting the backs of her fingers brush that delicious chest hair, making him moan when she tweaked his nipples, but he stayed still as she glided her fingertips over his flat stomach. She rested her hands there and rolled her hips, feeling the heat of his cock beneath the fabric, feeling the pulse and twitch of it. Okay, teasing him could be fun, especially since he'd made her work for this. She glanced up to see his wrists straining against the belt.

"Don't hurt yourself. You don't want to have to explain marks on your arms tomorrow."

He scowled. "You're going to make me come in my pants like a high school boy."

She eased back to look into his eyes and stroked her pussy against the placket of his pants again, making them both groan. "Really?"

"Paige, I'm too old for a dry hump. Take off my pants."

She bent forward, brushing her breasts against his bare chest as she kissed his throat, savoring the salty taste of him. She rubbed her mound against him through his pants, so close to orgasm herself, but wanting to make him lose control. He clenched his teeth, breathing fast as he growled her name, the word rumbling in his chest. God, he felt so good beneath her, hot and hard. She moved faster, her own need for orgasm making her mindless, greedy, as he thrust his hips up and shouted, his cock jerking beneath her. She rolled her hips as she sought her own pleasure, finding the tip of him through the fabric and rubbing until her climax shot through her. She dropped her head to his chest as the gentle pulses flowed through her, weakening muscles, relaxing nerves.

He bucked up against her as if trying to dislodge her. "What the hell? Christ, Paige."

Oh, he was pissed. She could feel it in his body that wasn't nearly as weak as hers. She lifted her head to grin at him. "I liked making you lose control. Think you can touch me now?" She reached over his head to tug at the end of the belt.

"You don't want me to touch you now," he said ominously.

She cocked her eyebrows, tracing the pattern of his chest hair. "I bet I do," she said when he drew a breath through his teeth.

"Let me go."

She shifted upward, sliding along his body, making him

groan. Unfastening the belt was a lot more complicated than tying him, because he'd pulled against it, and as she'd predicted, his wrists were red. She caressed the irritation before she found herself on her back beneath him.

"Want me to tie you up?" he growled.

"Decidedly not." She stroked her fingers through his hair, something she'd wanted to do for years. Just as thick and soft as she'd imagined. The tightness in his jaw told her he was considering it anyway, but instead he slid his hand down the front of her skirt, making her bow into his touch, before he closed his fingers around her hem and yanked it up.

She didn't recognize the strangled sound that came from her throat as he brushed his fingertips lightly across her mound, making her pussy quiver, her clit pulse. He barely touched the groomed curls, and his lips twitched in a smile when she lifted her hips toward his touch.

"What?"

"You just came, didn't you?" His touch hovered over her pussy.

"But you didn't make me come."

"What were you doing at the club tonight, Paige?" he asked, deliberately parting her thighs.

She trembled as he bared her vulnerable flesh to his view, his touch. "Looking for you."

His eyebrows winged up in surprise. "Is that right?" He stroked a line up the inside of her thigh, stopping just below where she wanted it, needed it.

"I heard—you went there." Her breath came in great pants now. "I wanted—" God, he kissed the inside of her knee. Who knew that would send a twinge of heat straight to her pussy?

"What did you want?" he asked, his deep voice sending another shiver through her.

"I wanted to see what turned you on."

His grip on her inner thigh tightened as he parted her legs wider and moved between them, still dressed, damn him. "What did you learn?"

"I can't—think when you're doing that."

"Doing what?" He caressed a circle high inside her other thigh and she felt a pulse of wetness slicken her pussy. "What turns me on?"

"Watching." She swallowed hard when he shifted his fingers to pass them back and forth over her mound, barely stirring the curls there, so close and yet, not what she needed. She forced herself to meet his gaze when she just wanted to sink her head back and give in to the sensation. "Two girls. Were you going to join them?"

"Would that have turned you on? What would you have done if you'd walked into the club to see me fucking someone else?"

Walked out again. She hated the burn of jealousy that accompanied the image. But she had to hide it, had to be sophisticated about her sexuality, or at least make him believe she was. "Maybe I would have watched."

His eyes darkened, for just a moment, before his grin flashed. "Liar." He lowered his mouth to kiss the area where he'd drawn the circle, letting his stubble heighten the sensation. "What turns you on, Paige?"

"That."

His mouth slid higher, and she whimpered when it rested just below the crease of her thigh. "Tell me what you want me to do to you."

She couldn't. The anticipation was delicious, and while she ached to come, she couldn't tell him which method she preferred, not when all options were so appealing. "I want you to do whatever you want."

"Now isn't that accommodating." He shifted his weight so

he was over her, his hands braced beside her shoulders, his nostrils flared as if taking in the scent of her arousal, his mouth so close. "You're usually bossy as hell."

"Kiss me," she managed.

His expression softened just a bit as he smoothed her hair back from her face and slanted his mouth over hers in the sweetest kiss she could imagine, his lips stroking, parting, his tongue feathering against the opening of her mouth before sliding deeper, tasting, savoring. God. She'd wanted this for so long, to be beneath him, to have him hold her, cradle her like she was something precious, for him to kiss her as though he'd wanted her forever too.

He eased back, looking at her. "I want to get you out of that dress."

Chapter Three

Paige scooted back to sit up without bumping heads with him. "You're still dressed," she pointed out.

"You first." He reached behind her for the zipper, not an easy task since the fabric was stretchy. But once the zipper made it to the middle of her back, he seemed satisfied, and drew the material away to bare her breasts. "Christ, Paige. You could turn me into a breast man. Gorgeous."

He cupped the full globes, his thumbs stroking over her nipples, tightening the already hard peaks until she ached for his mouth. Before she could voice her desire, he bent his head, first nuzzling her throat, nipping her collarbone, then sweeping down the slope of her breast to sip her nipple between his lips.

The cry that tore from her was rough as she let her head fall back. She twisted her fingers in his hair, holding him, bringing him closer, urging him to suck harder. He rolled the nipple against the roof of his mouth and scraped his teeth over it. She cried out again, wanting to press his hand between her thighs and come with her breast in his mouth.

Instead he sat up, releasing her breast with a pop. The expression on his face was unreadable, or at least she didn't want to read it, wanted to just drag his head down to her other breast and make him do it again.

"Take the dress off, Paige."

She wanted to scramble to do his bidding but had to remind herself she was sophisticated. That's what he wanted, right? She edged back a little more, because it wouldn't be very sophisticated to smack him in the nose as she wriggled out of the dress and tossed it over the nearby chair. She turned to him, completely naked.

This time his kiss didn't start gentle. He cupped the back of her neck to angle her head up to him and crushed her lips beneath his, as if he was angry with her for making him want her. But while the kiss was intense, it was also sexy as hell, his tongue stroking deep, his teeth catching her tongue when she dared to counter.

"Turn over," he said against her mouth, releasing her and sitting back on his knees.

She hid the disappointment that flashed through her. In her fantasies, they'd made love face to face, and he'd seen she was the only woman in the world he needed. But she did as he asked, kneeling and resting her hands on the pillows. The heat of his still-clothed body hovered over her as he braced his arms on either side of her waist, and his breath against her back sent tingles along her skin. He pressed a kiss to the indentation of her spine between her shoulder blades, and she gasped, not prepared for the eroticism of his caress. He moved to the middle of her back, and dragged his stubbled chin down her spine to the cleft of her ass. The sensation stole the breath from her body, making her light-headed. She dropped her head to the pillow and lifted her hips, encouraging another caress. He chuckled and eased back, framing her ass in his palms. His breath warmed her skin before he kissed the soft flesh there, teeth scraping, and he kissed the crease of skin between her butt and thigh. She gasped as pleasure pulsed through her, sending more wetness flowing from her pussy. She wanted his touch, his cock, something to relieve the building pressure in her cunt.

"Make me come," she moaned, turning her head against the pillow.

He sat up, no longer touching her, and she twisted to look at him.

"What?"

He unfastened his slacks. "On your back."

Her emotions jumbled. He'd aroused her, made her ready to be fucked from behind, and now he wanted her to face him. Now she could kiss him, hold him, while he made love to her. And God, she wanted to touch him. She rolled onto her back and sat up in the same movement.

"Let me," she said, reaching for his zipper, letting her fingers trace the line of his erection through his slacks.

He drew in a breath through his teeth that told her he didn't want to play around, so she opened his pants and reached inside. This time she drew in a breath. She'd gotten the impression he was big, the way he'd rubbed against her, but damn. Her cunt squeezed even as she worried about taking him into her.

"Don't tease," he chided softly as she glided her palm up the underside of his cock to slide her fingers around the head of him.

She released him and shoved his open slacks down his hips. He rose onto his knees to help her, then shifted to strip his slacks over his long lean legs. At last they were naked together, like she'd dreamed since she knew what sex was, only Zach was much bigger, muscular, broad shouldered than she'd fantasized, black hair across his hard pecs, and a cock dreams were made of, long and thick and dark with arousal. She curled her fingers around it, sliding up and down. He stretched out beside her, reaching for the wallet he'd tossed on the nightstand.

"I hope you have more than one," she murmured when he drew out his condom.

"Maybe once will be enough," he teased.

She tightened her grip around the base of his shaft. "I don't think so."

He tore open the packet and passed the condom to her. Her pulse kicked hard. He guided her as she fit it over the tip of his penis and rolled it down the length, securing it. He removed her touch and stroked her hair back from her face, bending to kiss her gently as he moved between her legs, his weight over her, his erection against her thighs. He glided his touch over her mound and parted her lips to stroke over her slick petals, God, finally, finally. She lifted her hips, parting her legs, inviting his fingers to explore, needing them to.

He slipped a finger into her, and another, thrusting, stretching until she pushed back. His jaw tightened, and he pushed deeper one more time before drawing his fingers free, sliding them up over her clit.

"I don't want to wait anymore." He shifted forward, pressing the head of his cock to her entrance, and flexed his hips, showing amazing restraint as he eased into her body.

Every centimeter of her channel fluttered with excitement at the invasion, at the slide and stretch. This was what she'd wanted for years. Zach over her, watching her, wanting her. She arched her back, bringing him deeper so his groin was flush against her pussy. She gasped at the sensation, and he smoothed his fingers over her cheek.

"Not very patient, are you?"

"I've waited long enough."

His eyes shuttered at that—when would she learn to keep her mouth shut?—and he curved his hands under her ass, stroking into her in little movements to keep himself deep. The thrusts bumped his groin against her swollen clit, and she was awash in pleasure and anticipation. She hoped the tightness of his expression had to do with him holding back his orgasm and not with her thoughtless words. She drew his head down to her, wanting his kiss. He covered her mouth with his, filling her with his taste, that expensive Scotch, his mouth moving in rhythm with his body, now slow and sultry, as if he, too, was absorbing every sensation.

She glided her palms over his back, feeling the muscles bunch and release with each thrust, feeling the power of him, the strength. God, he was beautiful, and tonight he was hers. She lightly scraped her nails over his buttocks and brushed the hair of his upper thighs. He made a sound, half grunt, half sigh in her ear, tensing over her.

"You have to—stop that."

She lifted her hands above his ass. "You don't like it?"

He rubbed his lips back and forth over her jaw. "I like it. Too much."

Delight shivered through her. "I thought old men like you couldn't come again so fast."

He pinched her ass. "Watch it, or I'll leave you in the dust."

She rolled her hips against his and trailed her fingers up his back to his shoulders, and down his arms, savoring the flex of muscles beneath her palms. "Your pride would never allow it."

"I don't like to be rushed."

She let her hands fall to the pillow beside her head, palms up in surrender. "By all means. Take your time."

He chuckled softly. The sound sent a thrill through her stronger than any caress, then disappeared as he lowered his head to her throat. She inclined her head back to allow him access as he nuzzled the sensitive underside of her jaw, stubble rasping, teeth scraping before his tongue soothed her skin. The attention tightened everything in her as he moved in and out of her with incredible control. He curved his hand under her breast to lift it to his mouth and teased her nipple with the lightest brush of his lips, the heat of his breath. She moaned and arched her back, inviting him to take more.

Instead he lifted his head, cupped the back of her knee and lifted her leg, bending it against her body, opening her wider for him, moving deeper, faster, more fully against her. His skin grew slick beneath her touch as she clutched his back. Each thrust, each pant that gusted over her flesh, brought her closer, closer, until her whole being focused on his cock, her clit. She thought she felt him swelling inside her. God, close.

He slipped his fingers between them and swept over her clit with dead accuracy, and she flew apart, the orgasm shooting through her, so strong she expected to see sparks shooting out the ends of her fingers. Zach's body strained against hers, pushing deep, flush against her, so close that she felt his heart pound all through her body. He groaned and stiffened with his release. His breath shuddered out of him as he lowered his head to her shoulder.

She curled her fingers through his hair and turned her head to kiss him, which he allowed about a second before he pulled away, out of her. She whimpered in protest when he rolled off the bed, but she was too boneless to reach for him. He moved to the bathroom in perfect naked glory, the man of her dreams. And she had to play it cool or tonight would be over before it had begun.

When Zach walked back into the room a few minutes later, Paige was curled on her side facing him, one hand propped under her head, still completely naked. He thought he'd battled his libido into submission, but his fingers itched to roam over that soft skin.

"Aren't you going to get dressed?" he asked, bending to reach for his pants.

"Why? Does this room rent by the hour?"

Smartass. "No. But don't you have to get home, get ready for work tomorrow?" He yanked on the pants sans underwear, needing some kind of barrier against her and her hungry gaze, as if she hadn't just melted in the orgasm he gave her minutes before.

"I'm good."

"Well. I have to be up early." He could leave. She could stay here tonight, and he could go home. But would he get any sleep thinking about what he'd walked away from?

"Then you should probably come to bed and get some sleep." She smoothed her hand on the duvet in front of her, on the bed that suddenly seemed too small.

"Put on some clothes."

Her mouth twisted in distaste. "That dress is itchy. I'd rather sleep naked. Unless you want to give me your shirt."

He scowled, but figured his shirt was safer than her bare skin, so he scooped it up and tossed it to her.

He couldn't take his gaze from her as she sat up, slipped it on and buttoned it up.

Ho. Ly. God.

Her breasts pushed against the fine white fabric, her nipples visible. The tails of the shirt covered her mons and ass but cut up high on her shapely legs. And knowing she was naked beneath made him hard.

Already.

And son of a bitch, she knew it. She knew just what she was doing to him as she lay back on the bed, arms stretched above her head, the lower placket of his shirt parting just over her pussy.

His head buzzing, he crossed to the phone and picked up the room-service menu beside it. "You want anything?" he asked.

"It's probably too late for room service."

How did she know that? How many hotel rooms had she been in? How many men had she been with? Rich, him wondering that, when he'd been with more women than he could count. He scanned the menu, anything to keep his eyes off her in that sultry pose.

"No, they serve until midnight. It's only a little after ten now." He extended the menu to her, but she shook her head. He set it back on the table, not hungry either. Well, hungry, but not for food.

"You don't have to sneak peeks, Zach. You are more than welcome to look." She drew up one leg so the fabric of his shirt fell away a little, exposing more of her cunt. "I want you to look. I want you to want me again."

He wanted her, no question. He shook with the desire. God, why was he so warped about this? He'd made love to her already. If he could just put all the complications of their relationship aside...

He sat on the edge of the bed, as far from her as he could get.

"You wouldn't have brought those girls here, right? You would have fucked them right there."

"Maybe. Or there are private rooms at the club."

"I'd heard that." She shifted on the bed but he didn't turn to look. "So why did you bring me here? Why didn't we just go in one of those rooms?"

"I don't know." He wasn't going to tell her she was too good for that place, that he'd wanted more privacy, more time. So why was he balking now, when he had all night, and she was clearly willing?

"You wanted me out of there."

He didn't answer.

"But you wanted me. Was it me you wanted, or would any girl there have done?"

He turned to her, saw her leg drawn up, damn near modest, though she looked like a model there in his shirt, sexy as fucking hell. "No. No girl there would have done."

The smile she gave him was the girl he'd known since she was nine, not the seductress, and she sat up, folding her legs in front of him. Thank God the shirttails fell between her parted thighs.

"I changed my mind. I want ice cream."

He studied her a moment to see if she was fucking with him. But she seemed perfectly innocent—at least as innocent as a woman wearing the shirt of the man she'd just made love to could look. He reached for the phone. "A sundae?"

Well. That was a bad decision. The server delivered a hot-fudge sundae that could feed a small city—the sink basin was smaller than the bowl. Paige took it with a moan of approval and settled in the center of the bed. Her expression of delight as she took the first bite drew him closer to the bed despite himself.

"You want some?"

"I'm not much of an ice cream guy." The whipped cream, though, that might be another story.

"Come on." She waved a spoonful of melting ice cream and fudge at him.

He shook his head, and she shrugged, directing the spoon to her own mouth. A dollop of chocolate dropped from her spoon, right to her cleavage.

"Oh!" She looked up at him with a wicked gleam in her eyes. "Cold!"

Yeah, he noticed, because her nipples were pushing against the fabric of his shirt, and he no longer cared that she was waving chocolate near the fine material. "I'll get a towel," he said, though his feet seemed to be rooted to the spot.

"That's okay." She reached between her breasts and

scooped the chocolate up with her finger, which she promptly thrust in her mouth, licking while she kept her gaze on him.

He was instantly hard, and she knew exactly what she was doing. She took another bite, this one actually making it in her mouth, but his gaze was riveted to the streak of chocolate on her skin just above the opening of his shirt. God, he needed to taste her. She took another big spoonful, smiling at him around it, and he knelt on the bed beside her, removing the bowl from her hands.

"Get out of my shirt before you get it dirty."

Tossing her hair back so she could look straight into his eyes, she lifted her fingers to the buttons and worked them free, baring all that smooth white skin. When his shirt was safely across the room, and she sat in the same position, one leg folded in front, the other behind, her head tilted up expectantly. He edged closer, dipping the spoon in the melting whipped cream and smearing it over her parted lips. She gasped when he bent to lick it off, slipping his tongue between her lips, stroking from the cool to the heat and feeling the vibration of her lust all the way to his cock.

He lifted his head, dug the spoon a bit deeper and coated it with the thick fudge. She drew in a breath as he dangled it over her before smearing it between her breasts. She let her head fall back on a moan, and he lowered his head to lick it from her skin, his tongue dragging slowly over her flesh as he braced his hand on the bed beside her. The chocolate combined with the saltiness of her skin, and the scent of her arousal. Christ. He didn't know how much longer he could play this game.

He straightened, swirled the spoon and touched it to her breast before sucking the sweet ice cream concoction from her taut nipple.

She slid her fingers down his arm and reached for the bowl, but he held it out of her reach.

"I'm not done yet. Lay back."

She did, a bit too eagerly, and parted her legs. He ground his teeth against the desire to toss the ice cream aside and fuck her, but he'd started this. And he loved the way she was going along with it, never taking her gaze from him as her skin flushed with desire, her breath growing shallow with it. He stroked the spoon over her flat stomach and followed the line from her ribs to her navel with his tongue. She curled her fingers in his hair, and he had the feeling she wanted to push him lower. Instead she held him while he lapped at her skin, her legs moving restlessly.

"I thought you didn't like ice cream."

"Never found the right combination before." He eased down over her thighs. "Spread your legs, Paige."

"Words I've wanted to hear from you for a long time." She did as he asked.

He paused, looking at her pretty pink pussy, swollen and slick. Setting the ice cream aside, he bent to tease her clit. The taste of her coated his tongue before he thrust it inside her. She moaned and wriggled beneath him, her fingers winding tightly in his hair. Without looking away from her, he reached for a glob of ice cream and dropped the cold sweet right on her clit.

She screamed and bucked up, offering it to him. How could he refuse? He closed his mouth around the treat and her clit, rolling the ice cream against her flesh as she pumped her hips, opening herself wider, wanting more.

He rose, looking up the length of her body at her parted lips, her dark eyes. She whimpered in protest when she realized he wasn't going to make her come. Instead he cupped the bowl to move it to the nightstand.

She wrapped her fingers around his wrist. "Not so fast. On your back."

Zach was torn. He wasn't wild about ice cream being spread over him, but the idea of her licking it off—yeah, okay. He turned onto his back, hands on the pillow beside him in surrender as she knelt over him, gorgeous breasts swaying with the movement. He gave in to the temptation to tug one nipple into hardness. She grinned and reached for the fastening of his pants. She made short work of them, freeing his erection and sliding her palm up and down it, just to make him crazy, no doubt. Then, tucking her wild curls behind her ear, she bent and closed her lips around the head of his cock.

Every ounce of will kept him from thrusting his hips upward to push deeper into her mouth, to fulfill this fantasy. But no, he'd let her take it slow, as long as it wasn't too slow. She parted her mouth wider to bring him deeper, her tongue sliding down the underside of him, teasing the bundle of nerves at the base of the head while her fingers closed around his shaft, pumping gently. He let out a groan through his teeth, and she looked up at him, eyes knowing, before she took more of him, her mouth hot and wet, sliding up and down, her gorgeous hair streaming over the tops of his thighs, tangling with the coarse hair there. The tip of him bumped the back of her throat, and she slid her mouth all the way up, releasing him with a pop.

And she reached for the bowl.

Alarm tripped his pulse. "I don't think that's a good idea."

Like she'd start listening to him now. She scooped a spoonful of the unmelted ice cream, waved it over his cock a couple of times before slipping the spoon between her own lips.

He barely had the chance to be relieved when she took him back into her mouth.

The cold ice cream touched the tender skin, and he sat up with a shout. But she didn't release him, only coated his shaft with the concoction, mouth working, the ice cream melting between her tongue and his skin. The combination of sensation was overwhelming, and Christ, he wanted to let go. But he hadn't let her come.

"Stop. Jesus. I want to be inside you."

Before he lost his mind completely to pleasure, he scrambled behind him for a condom from the nightstand and shoved it at her. She took it, and with one last stroke of her lips on him, sat back to open the condom.

She took her sweet time about it too, and he was about to snatch it away when she settled her knees on either side of his hips and rolled it on, then guided him to her entrance and into her.

His fingers dug into her hips so hard he saw white spots on her skin. His balls were tight, ready for the orgasm that he fought to hold in.

Finally she started moving over him, her palm in the center of his chest, her hair and breasts swaying with her movements, the sexiest goddamned thing he'd ever seen. His gaze was drawn to her pussy swallowing his cock. Her rhythm was exquisite, and a fine sheen of sweat coated her skin.

"Touch yourself," he urged, his voice almost unrecognizable.

Her eyes brightened. She reached for his hand and placed it on hers. "Show me."

She was a fantasy come true. God help him. He guided her hand over her breast, coaxing her fingers to pinch her already-erect nipple. He urged it down her flat belly to toy in her curls, no longer neat. He watched her eyes heat as he slicked her fingers over her clit, and felt her pussy squeeze around him.

"Make yourself come," he said, pushing his hips against hers, his cock deeper into her heat. God, he wished he could feel her naked around him, but he had to protect her. "Come for me, Paige."

He watched as her fingers flicked and swirled around the pulsing bud. Her rhythm became erratic as she saw to her own pleasure, so he put his hands on her hips again and took over, pushing little pants from her as her fingers played over her clit.

Her orgasm was as gorgeous as she was, her body bowing back, her skin flushing, breasts high, fingers moving with a sensuous rhythm now, drawing out every molecule of pleasure as her channel clasped around him. Only then did he release his own orgasm with a shout, grinding up, feeling her drench his balls.

She collapsed over him, her fingers twining through his on the mattress as her cheek pressed against his pounding heart. He stroked her sweat-slickened back, then eased his hand up to toss her hair off her neck to cool her. He couldn't get enough of touching her, damn it. All that silky skin, gorgeous breasts, long legs. He'd known this was a mistake from the beginning, but he hadn't realized how quickly she would get under his skin.

Chapter Four

Paige glided her fingertips in circles over Zach's palm and listened to his heartbeat slow to normal. Amazing to think she could have made this man come three times tonight, each time as eagerly as the last. She felt powerful, sexy, strong.

He shifted beneath her and curved his hands over her shoulders. "I need to get up, take care of this."

The condom, he meant. Reluctantly she slid to her side facing him, watching the play of muscles in his back, ass and legs as he rolled off the bed and walked to the bathroom. God, he was beautiful. Longing tugged deep within her. Yes, she might have him in her bed now, but it wouldn't last. She knew what he wanted out of life, and falling in love wasn't it. No matter what she might do to convince him she was the one for him, he wouldn't see it.

So she'd take what she could get and nurse her broken heart tomorrow.

She heard the shower turn on and forced her limp muscles to sit up. She was feeling a little sticky from the ice cream that now sat as slush in the bowl. She made her way across the carpet, feeling twinges in places she'd never twinged before. Right. Two rounds of lovemaking, no matter how hot, had after-effects.

She tested the doorknob and found it unlocked, so opened it and stepped in.

She hadn't seen the bathroom when they came in, but it was roomy, with a separate tub, and the shower behind glass blocks. She indulged herself with watching the blurred shape of Zach through them, before she stepped forward.

Water streamed over his face, flattening his hair, sluicing over his brow as he stood with one hand braced against the wall.

"Room for two?" she asked, and he whipped around, swiping the water from his eyes.

She wouldn't let his reaction chase her off. If tonight was all she had, she was going to make the most of it.

"I have ice cream in interesting places," she said, edging past him to steal some of the spray, while he watched her warily.

"You're going to have bruises on your hips," he said, his voice echoing off the glass. "I'm sorry."

She coasted her palms down her reddened skin. "It's fine. No one will see." She considered, then tilted her head back under the water. Her makeup and hair-styling product were probably all sweated off anyway. She lifted her head again to see him staring at her. "What? Raccoon eyes?"

He shook his head, his jaw tight, and for a moment, she thought he'd bolt. Instead, he stepped forward, scooped her hair back from her face and kissed her.

The kiss was everything she'd dreamed of, gentle yet passionate, as if he craved her beyond anything, his lips gliding over hers, tongue stroking her lower lip, his lips covering hers, parting hers, to dip inside, filling her with his taste. She slid her fingers over his chest, the hair there rasping her palms, up to his broad, muscular shoulders, down his arms. Their bodies didn't touch, only their mouths and hands.

He released her and stepped out of the shower, leaving her alone and confused.

When she joined him a few minutes later, dry and wrapped in a hotel robe, he was beneath the sheets, bare-chested, his hair damp from the shower. A quick glance around the room told her he was naked—his pants were draped over a chair, his boxers folded beside them. She toweled the underside of her hair as she considered. She'd never spent the night with a guy in a hotel before. What was the etiquette?

He turned his gaze to her. "Do you want to watch some television or something?"

She shook her head and tossed the towel back in the direction of the bathroom. He followed the path and winced when it landed. Of course. She'd forgotten how fastidious he was. But she gained his attention quickly when she shrugged out of her robe and crossed the room to the opposite side of the bed. She lifted the sheets enough to confirm her suspicion that he was indeed naked, and slipped in beside him.

"You're warm," she murmured, and wondered how he'd react if she cuddled up against him.

He twisted toward the nightstand, and she hoped he was reaching for another condom. Instead, he picked up his phone. "What time do you need to be up?"

Right. Work tomorrow. Considering she had nothing but her sexy evening dress, not even underwear, no makeup and her hair would look like a rat's nest in the morning— "I'd better leave here about seven."

He nodded and set the phone down without changing anything. "I have the alarm set for six thirty. Good enough?"

Such an odd conversation to have with the man of her fantasies while naked in bed with him. "Sure."

She settled uncertainly on the pillow facing him. What now? Small talk? Sleep? Could she sleep with him an arm's length away?

He shifted onto his side to face her, and almost as if he couldn't help himself, stroked her bare arm above the sheet. "Matt asked me to be in the wedding party."

She smiled. Right. They knew how to talk to one another. They'd known each other for fifteen years. "Technically it's a commitment party. Good. Are you going to?"

His gaze flicked from following his hand on her arm to her face. "Sure. Why not?"

"Because to hear you tell it, you're not all that into commitment, no matter what type."

He flinched. "My commitment. I'm fine with Matt's."

"They're very happy."

"Yeah, I know." His fingers traveled up to twine in her curls. "Are you in the commitment party?"

"Already have my dress."

"I hope it starts at your chin and goes to the floor, because if Adam sees me looking at you—"

She turned her mouth down in an exaggerated pout. "You won't look at me otherwise?"

"Not if I treasure my balls. And I do."

She wouldn't let his words sting, would play it off as she always had—teasing him. "So you won't look at me under miles of fabric and remember what I looked like tonight, straddling you, my legs spread for your mouth, my—"

He covered her mouth with his palm, his expression pained. "I will not. And you won't look at me like you want me to remember that."

She pushed his hand away and leaned closer. "The dress is actually cut down to here." She motioned just below her breasts. "And cut high enough on the side to have easy access."

He grimaced and rolled onto his back, reaching for the bedside lamp. "Go to sleep, Paige."

Paige woke to the sound of the hotel alarm and slid her hand across the mattress. Cool. Her eyes popped open. He was gone. No real surprise—he'd been on edge all night, even when he'd been making love to her, and he hadn't drawn her into his arms afterwards, soothed her to sleep. She ignored the twinge of regret. She'd known what she was doing last night.

She flipped on the bedside lamp, just to make sure, holding the sheets to her breast, more out of security than modesty. After all, no one was here but her. His clothes were gone. In their place was a bag from a 24-hour discount store. Curiosity driving her, she got out of bed to open it. Inside were toothpaste and a toothbrush, a pair of panties, jeans, a bra and a T-shirt. Great. She wouldn't have to make the walk of shame in last night's dress. The effort touched her.

Then she saw the envelope at the bottom of the bag.

She recognized his scrawl on the front, squinted to decipher.

"Didn't know if you brought your car. Money in here for a cab ride home. Room's paid for."

Nothing else, no see you soon or call you later. Her stomach tightened in disappointment, though she couldn't say she'd expected more. Hoped, yes, but the logical part of her had known it would happen like this. She rose and dressed in her new clothes, a hair too big. She tucked last night's dress in the bag, wrapped it up as small as she could, and headed out, head held high.

Zach stared at the computer screen without seeing the ad displayed there for his approval.

He'd left Paige in a hotel room with cash and clothes from a 24-hour store. She may have pretended to come to him a sex-sophisticate, determined to show him she could be as casual about their intimacy as he, but he knew better. He'd seen the adoration in her eyes, and Jesus, he'd liked it. He couldn't remember the last time he'd been adored. And damn it, he hadn't deserved it, had been all uptight and snarly, as if touching her, making love to her, was the last thing he wanted. He was good at sex, he had fun with it, but other than the bit with the ice cream, he hadn't shown her that side of him. He hated himself for that almost as much as he did for leaving her alone.

But no, he couldn't think about that any more than he could think about touching her creamy skin or her wild hair, any more than he could think about the taste of her mouth, the sound of her sighs. She wanted something more, and he had no desire to enter a relationship with her, or any woman, not for a good long time.

The buzz of his phone jolted him out of his thoughts, and he glanced down at the display. For a split second he hoped it would be Paige, reading him the riot act he deserved.

But it was worse—Adam's name glared from the screen.

Fuck.

He swallowed, took a deep breath and answered. "Hey, man."

"Hey, ladies' night at Queenie's tonight."

Zach's stomach unknotted momentarily as he realized Adam hadn't learned about him and Paige. No, who was he kidding? If Adam found out, he'd march down here and personally rip Zach's dick off. After relief—or something like it—set in, he could focus on Adam's invitation. The last thing he wanted was to see Adam face to face. The minute his friend looked at him, he'd know. Zach wasn't accustomed to keeping secrets from his best friend, but his life kinda depended on him keeping this one.

"Yeah, I'm not really up for it." Even as he said it, he knew the words sounded lame.

"What the hell? Not up for it?" Adam's question was a taunt. "Since when? We're talking Queenie's, with the prettiest girls in the city."

"Yeah, not—" He cleared his throat. "May be coming down with something."

"Fuck. You've met somebody. The last time you were too sick to go out, you were banging that Jill chick from your office."

Zach winced. The downside to a lifelong friendship was that your friend knew every secret, and worse, knew when you were lying. Still, he tried. "Yeah, no, not this time. I just need to get out of here and get some rest. And, you know, not spread my germs all over Queenie's."

"Right. Whatever. But if I hook up with two ladies, you have to listen to every detail."

Zach disconnected and sat back in his chair, dragging his hands down his face. He had a reprieve.

Only not going out meant staying in. Zach couldn't remember the last time he'd done that. His apartment was great, the best tech, comfortable stylish furniture, but despite its spaciousness, he felt boxed in with his thoughts.

Mostly about Paige, mostly about last night, each aspect running through his mind with the commentary of a Monday-morning quarterback. How sexy she'd been, how soft, how willing, and what a dick he'd been.

He should call and apologize. If she hung up on him, well, he'd have tried, right? She hadn't deserved to be treated like that, and maybe if he knew he'd never see her again, he'd have let it go. But he would be seeing her again at the commitment ceremony, so best to clear the air now, let her tear into him in private instead of in front of her whole family.

With that in mind, he picked up his car keys. Seeing her face to face could have its complications—like projectiles thrown at his head—but it might make her feel better.

And part of him wanted to see her really, really pissed.

His good intentions fled when she opened the door. Surprise flitted across her face, followed by pleasure. When a smile started to curve her lips, all bets were off. He cupped her head in his hand as he brought his mouth down to hers. The taste of her flooded his senses—she'd been drinking wine, and the sharp taste combined with her softer one. He let his desire carry him through the door, bumping them both into a table and knocking things over, lifting her onto it and pressing his hips between her knees to part them, needing to get closer.

Only then did he register the distressed sound to his right. Not from Paige, who was clutching his shoulders and kissing him back, but from a short distance away. He released Paige's mouth and reluctantly turned his head to find the source.

A small girl, maybe four or five years old, stood in her nightgown at the end of the hallway with her finger in her mouth and tears streaming down her cheeks. Paige came to her senses and shoved his shoulders. He stepped back to release her, and she pushed past him to go to the child, who she swept up in her arms, one hand cradling, the other soothing, stroking the curly reddish-brown hair.

"Oh, sweetie, I thought you were watching TV. It's okay."

Seeing Paige comfort the child brought a deeper ache to his gut. Something he'd never felt before and wouldn't even know how to name.

"He wasn't hurting me, CeCe. It's okay. It's okay. Don't cry." She bounced the child in her arms as Zach tried to reason out what had happened here.

"Is she yours?" he managed, taking in the curly hair on both females, though CeCe's was softer and lighter.

She looked at him. Irritation darkened her eyes and hardened the line of her lips. "My roommate's daughter." She kept her tone soft, for the child, he imagined.

He moved toward her, stretching a hand out, though he wasn't sure what he could do to comfort the girl. "Sorry. I didn't mean to scare her. I was just thinking—"

"I know what you were thinking."

Yep, definitely irritated. He let his arm fall to his side. "I didn't know."

"You might have thought about whether or not I was alone before you charged in here." Still that soothing tone that didn't mask the bite of her words. She set the child down, but the girl still clung to Paige's leg, her baleful attention on Zach. "You might have thought about your welcome."

A grin hooked up the corner of his mouth, though he saw right away that was a mistake. Paige narrowed her eyes.

"I'm sorry. I was—stupid."

She lifted her eyebrows. "Elaborate, please."

He'd come here to make his mea culpas, and probably should have started with that, instead of the lip-lock when he walked in. But the words he'd planned to say had been shoved back by the kiss. "I'm sorry I left you alone. That wasn't the right thing to do."

"I imagine you do it a lot, though. Wait until the girl goes to sleep, then slip out?"

He winced. "Usually the sleeping part doesn't come into play," he said, since he'd chosen honesty. "We part after the—activities." He cast a cautious look at CeCe, who still glared at him. Hopefully she couldn't follow this conversation.

"And?"

Right. And. "I shouldn't have left. I shouldn't have barged in. Anything else I shouldn't have done?"

"You shouldn't have brought that attitude."

He sighed. "All right. I'm sorry. A lot. I should have said goodbye. I should have called."

"But you didn't because—?"

"Because I don't. I don't stay, I don't get involved. I tried to tell you, so why were you surprised?" He hated the defensive tone in his own voice. He'd come here to apologize, not defend his actions, definitely not to turn it around on her.

Paige tossed her hair back over her shoulders, her hand moving over the girl's small back. "You're here," she pointed out.

He was here. He could have called but he'd come over. And worse, he'd kissed her, let the hunger he'd been feeling since he left the hotel room take over his sense of self-preservation. The best thing to do was to say his piece, let her rake him over the coals some more, and get the hell out. Then it would be over. But he couldn't make himself move toward the door.

She looked past him to the entryway table, with its tumbled picture frames and the mail dumped on the floor. "That's why you came?"

He bent to scoop the mail off the floor and stacked it neatly on the table before setting the frames to rights. Pictures of CeCe, mostly, with a lovely blonde who must be her mother. One of Paige with her brothers that had Zach swallowing.

"You didn't come because you think I'm going to tell Adam, did you?"

He snapped his gaze to hers. The thought hadn't even occurred to him, but she probably wouldn't believe that. "Of course not. You're not ten years old anymore."

She eyed him as if she didn't quite believe him. "What are you going to do to make it up to me?"

He cast a teasing glance at the table where he'd kissed her.

She frowned and jammed her hand on her hip. Sexiest thing he'd ever seen. But the message was clear. Fat chance. Something rose up in him that completely erased his need to escape. Something stronger than his long-ingrained need to protect his privacy. But it wasn't just desire, either. It was foreign to him.

"Are you free for dinner?" The question surprised him the minute it was out of his mouth.

Her eyes widened, letting him know she hadn't expected it, either. "It's after eight. And I'm babysitting."

"Right." He looked from the suspicious child to the equally suspicious woman. "When are you done?"

"Her mom works until two. So a while."

"Ah." He backed toward the still-open door. His chance to escape, though it no longer had the same appeal. "Tomorrow?"

She ushered the child into the room behind her—the living room, he reasoned—and cocked a hip. "You came here to see me, right? Otherwise you'd just have called."

His defenses went up. He didn't want her to look too closely at his motivations, especially when he wasn't sure what they were. And yes, he had wanted to see her again, to remind himself what a bad idea his continuing fantasies were. "If I didn't think you'd hang up on me. Or ignore the phone altogether."

"Then stay."

Panic tripped his pulse. He glanced past her to the room where the kid had disappeared. "Help you babysit?" That sounded so damned domestic.

"You can't tell me you've never done that before."

"Oh, I definitely have." Years ago, with Becky Turner, the girl who gave him his first blowjob. Not that he thought Paige would do the same, but the possibility of it, the idea of being near her held more appeal than he wanted to admit. He closed the door and moved nearer. Before he could touch her, and God, he ached to touch her, she spun and entered the room after CeCe. The little girl was curled up on the deep-green sofa in the cozy little room, and held up a DVD case for Paige. Paige took it and loaded the player beneath a small flat-screen TV.

"Just fifteen minutes, okay? It's past your bedtime."

As Paige got the child comfortable, Zach looked around. The furnishings were modern, if modest, the wall behind the couch painted a soothing creamed-coffee color, and iron accents decorated the room. The signs of a kid living here were the collection of G-rated movies in the black cabinet beneath the TV and the pile of pillows and stuffed animals on the floor.

"Does she talk?" He eyed the girl with the same wariness she eyed him.

"Of course she talks. Just not to strangers. CeCe, this is my friend Zach. He's not a bad guy."

"So why are you mad at him?" CeCe asked around the fingers in her mouth.

"Because he doesn't make good decisions. Just like Mommy gets mad at you when you do something you know you shouldn't do."

CeCe's frown deepened. "What did he do?"

Zach watched Paige as she thought about how to explain his mistakes to a little kid.

"He broke a promise."

Huh. He didn't see that coming. What promise?

"What promise?" CeCe echoed his thoughts.

Paige flushed. "Your movie's starting." She settled on the couch and Zach crossed to sit beside her, not as easily distracted.

"What promise?"

"Not spoken," she said, her gaze on the TV. "But you know what you did."

"I'm sorry, Paige. I acted on impulse."

She turned to him. "Why? Did you think Adam had a tracking device on me and he was going to storm in at any minute?"

"I don't know." He passed a hand over his hair and rested his elbow on his knees.

She wasn't completely satisfied, he could tell by the set of her lips. She turned away, hugging a pillow to her. He wished he was that pillow. He had a lot of groveling to do first before she'd let him that close again. If tonight showed him anything, it was that he wanted back in her bed. And if he was going to do that...he was opening himself up to a relationship. Funny how sitting on the couch with her curled beside him didn't make that seem like such a bad thing. While he was content with his life, he wasn't a man who sought comfort. But here with Paige he could see the benefits of it, if he was another kind of man. She was a woman who wanted a relationship, and he was a man who avoided them.

As the animated movie turned to a live-action film, he reached over to touch one of Paige's curls, half-expecting her to swat his hand away. Instead, she allowed it for a moment, then angled her head to break the contact. But she didn't chase him out, and fifteen minutes later, she made good on her bargain. CeCe argued, but only a little, as Paige shut off the TV, bent to wrap the girl's arms around her neck and lifted her from the floor.

That sensation again, like hunger, but not. Something primal but unrecognizable.

"I'll be right back," she told Zach, and slipped into the other room.

After a few minutes—was she singing? Maybe reading—she emerged and sat on the couch beside him, closer this time, and swept her hair over her shoulder, exposing that gorgeous throat. Did she know the invitation she was sending? He rested his arm over the cushion of the couch behind her, and she didn't move away. Okay, she knew.

"I'm sorry, Paige," he murmured, and with his finger under her chin, tilted her mouth up to meet his.

He kept the kiss sweet, his lips fitting over hers, taking her soft sigh into his mouth as their mouths moved together in a gentle rhythm, nothing like his greeting at the door, just following the shape of her lips, ignoring the tentative caress of her tongue, focusing on the kind of kiss they might see if they watched CeCe's movie to the end.

Paige shifted, cupping the back of his head. She slanted her lips over his, parting them, her tongue teasing, drawing his out. He deepened the kiss, turning to press her against the back of the couch. Her touch moved restlessly over his shoulders and along his spine, and he parted her thighs with his knee, ready to press against the heat of her body.

Just like that, she broke the kiss. "I think you should probably go now."

His hormones soaked that in, his gaze moving from her mouth to her eyes. Okay. Not kidding. He eased away, trying to convince his erection that nothing was happening tonight. He drew a deep breath, one arm braced on the arm of the couch as he studied their reflection in the dark TV screen.

"Right," he said when it didn't appear she was going to change her mind. "Okay." He stood and wiped his palms down the front of his jeans. "Are you free for dinner tomorrow?"

She angled her head to look up at him. "Just dinner."

Just—he hadn't had "just dinner" with a woman in years. If a woman wanted "just dinner" he steered clear. But this was Paige. She wanted to be romanced. And, after seeing her again, being here with her, he wanted her back in his bed. Right now, no other woman would do. Despite the ache in his groin, he nodded. No matter how stupid this might be, Zach always went after what he wanted.

Chapter Five

As she waited for Zach to pick her up for their date, Paige's stomach fluttered more than it had when she'd walked into the sex club the other night. She'd thought long and hard about their first night together, both at the club and at the hotel. Zach was attentive, and made her feel like the only woman in the world—while he was inside her. But before, and after, left her feeling as lonely and empty as the bed when she woke up.

She wanted more, and she wanted it from Zach. Yes, he was handsome, and yes, a kind of power rolled through her when she thought about being the woman to tame his wild ways. She'd watched him grow up the middle child in a struggling family of five children, watched him study hard to get a scholarship to college, the first in his family to make it there. She could understand his need to indulge himself after that. But she also knew he had more to offer.

She needed to see what he was willing to give, because she was prepared to hand over her heart.

The kiss last night had been toe-curlingly romantic and sexy, and that he hadn't argued when she asked him to stop gave her hope. It wasn't enough that he see her as a grown woman. She wanted him to fall in love with her.

When the doorbell rang, she answered. Her breath caught to see him standing in the hallway dressed in a business suit, head dipped, just a touch of five o'clock shadow. His gaze slid over her and warmed appreciatively as he took in her flowy white dress and sandals.

"You look gorgeous," he said in that voice that sent shivers down her spine.

"Thanks. So do you." Okay, her breathless voice didn't bode well for him seeing her as a grown woman. She reached for her purse on the table behind her. "Shall we go?"

"That's not what happened," Zach said with a disbelieving laugh, setting his wine glass at the far edge of his plate on the white tablecloth.

Paige couldn't remember the last time she'd heard him laugh like that, and she hadn't seen him so relaxed since they'd encountered one another again. She'd take responsibility for that—she hadn't made life easy for him once she'd set her sights on him. Maybe he was worried about Adam and his reaction. She understood the whole big-brother thing, but she wasn't going to let what Adam thought get in the way of her desire. And she wanted Zach more than anything.

"So explain to me why you were sitting outside my senior prom, hunkered down in your car." She'd noticed his car the moment she'd walked out of the country club where the prom had been held. Her heart had done a little jump at the sight. Even then he'd been so gorgeous.

The corners of his lips turned down as he turned the wine glass on the table, his attention focused on the wavy liquid. "Adam asked me to look out for you."

"Why wasn't he there?"

"He was up on The Hill, waiting to stop you if you got past me."

The Hill had been where kids had gone to park their cars and make out in those days. More than one person she'd known had ended up pregnant after a night in the backseat. Her friends had declared it cursed and never let their guys get their panties off after that. "What made him think if I was planning to sleep with Chris, that I'd do it up on The Hill? What about a motel room? Didn't he think of that?" Which had been the plan, until she saw Zach's car and had crossed the lot to show her displeasure at his imposition by banging on the hood and yelling at him for invading her privacy—though part of her romantic young heart had allowed her to believe jealousy on his part motivated his actions. Poor Chris. She'd been on a tear about nosey family members, and he'd ended up just taking her home.

"I think your dad had that angle covered, threatening any motel owners that offered Chris a room."

She flipped her hair over her shoulder. "You were too late in any case. I lost my virginity way before senior prom."

Zach snapped his gaze to hers. "You did?" His tone was sharp, fatherly. "With who?"

"Jordan, two days after my sixteenth birthday."

He snorted. "Jordan was a dick. I'm sure it was very memorable for you."

"I remember locking myself up in the bathroom afterwards." The night before she gave in to Jordan's pleadings, Zach had turned up at the house, home from college break, and hadn't looked at her, though she'd teased him, practically begging for his attention. When he'd brushed her off, her fragile young heart had been broken, and she decided she needed to grow up, so she'd given in to Jordan. And for the two minutes he'd been inside her, she'd imagined he was Zach. She'd continued that practice well into college before she realized she was cheating herself.

"I'd like to kick his ass for even looking at you," Zach said, his voice a low rumble.

She gave him an exaggerated pout through her lashes. "Why? I was cute, and I wanted someone to look at me."

His lips curved down and his eyebrows drew together. "You were too young, and Jordan didn't know what he was doing."

She folded her arms on the table and watched his gaze flick to her cleavage. "How old were you when you lost your virginity?"

The corner of his mouth lifted. "Sixteen, but I knew what I was doing."

She rolled her eyes. "You do now, but I doubt you did then."

"I did. I could give you references." He winked, and delight raced through her at the lighthearted gesture.

"No thank you." She sat back and folded her hands primly on the table in front of her. "And I'd appreciate you not giving out my name as a reference in the future."

He chuckled, the low sound sending a thrill through her. "I'd be too afraid of what you'd say about me."

She angled her head, determined to keep the mood playful. "Which would hurt worse, a comment about size or endurance?"

The waiter, who'd chosen that moment to reach for her water glass, lifted his eyebrows, filled the glass and moved on.

"Why are we talking about sex?" he asked. "Are you trying to make me crazy?"

"That has long been my favorite pastime."

"Sex? Or making me crazy?"

She let her lips curve in a mysterious smile. "Wouldn't you like to know?"

He lifted her hand from the table and rubbed his thumb over her knuckles. "What are we doing here?"

"We're on a date."

"Why?"

"Because I figured since I already put out, you could buy me dinner."

The waiter, passing by, almost tripped over his own shoelaces.

"So we're doing this backwards." He placed her hand on the table and rubbed his palms on the arms of the chair as if he had to touch something.

"Roundabout, maybe. I don't usually move in a straight line." She held her hand out expectantly, and he put his in hers. She turned it over, palm up, and traced a circle on his palm, then a figure eight, and watched his nostrils flare as he followed her movement. "I don't want any dessert."

The words were barely out of her mouth before his free hand shot into the air, signaling for the check.

Zach pressed her against the wall outside the door of her apartment, unable to keep his hands from her any longer, coursing his palms down her sides and up, over her hips, lifting her skirt a few inches as he explored her mouth with his tongue, as her fingers curled into his hair, holding him to her, her kiss as hungry as his. He pressed his erection into the softness of her belly, needing the contact, needing her to see what she did to him, and she rubbed back. God, yes. He groaned into her mouth, and she broke the kiss, turning in his arms to fumble for her keys in the light by the door. The jangle of metal was almost an aphrodisiac. Soon he'd be in her apartment, in her bed, in her body. The key slid in the lock, and he turned to follow, only to have her stop in the open doorway, her hand braced on the door-frame as she faced him.

"Good night," she murmured, and closed the door.

He stared a few moments, waiting for her to open it again, then he heard the chain. Well, hell. She couldn't have picked a worse punishment for his crime.

The quiet knock on Paige's door the next morning surprised her. She set her cup of coffee on the breakfast bar and crossed the room to peek through the peephole.

Her heart kicked when she saw Zach. This was twice he'd shown up of his own volition. What did that mean? Probably that he was as determined to get her back in bed without falling in love with her as she was determined to get him to fall in love with her before they got back in bed.

She removed the chain and opened the door. He bounced on the balls of his feet in a T-shirt and running shorts.

"Want to go for a run with me? We can get coffee afterwards."

A run. She didn't run. She'd planned to hit the gym downstairs in a few minutes, so was already in her yoga pants and tank top, but running? That was outside, and jarring, and she was pretty sure Zach wouldn't find her wheezing sexy. But no way was she sending him off, not when he'd gone to the effort, clearly wanting to spend time with her, no matter his motivation.

"We could swim. There's no one at the apartment pool this early, and it's great to do laps."

Wariness tightened his features. "You'd be wearing a bathing suit, I'd imagine."

She cocked her hip. "I'm not quite daring enough to go without."

"It's probably not one of those that covers you chin to knee."

She had several bathing suits, in fact. One was a modest exercise suit—well, as modest as it could be for a woman with boobs like hers. And she had a tiny bikini that looked like crochet. Of course she would wear that one for Zach, even if it was harder to swim laps in. "It's a two-piece."

He swallowed, and she could see he was making an effort not to look below her chin. "You're trying to kill me."

Test him, at the very least. She stepped back to invite him in. "Help yourself to the coffee. I'm going to change."

Zach was glad he hadn't taken a sip of coffee when Paige walked out of the bedroom, wearing nothing but strategically placed strings over her full breasts and hips. Her skin was smooth, and he closed his hand against the remembered sensation of it, at the remembered response when he'd stroked it. He was insane for agreeing to this, when it couldn't end well.

The worst of it was, he wasn't being led by his dick, not entirely. He'd had a good time at dinner. While, yes, part of his mind had been on taking her to bed, he'd otherwise been relaxed. He hadn't been the successful ad exec or the charming ladies' man, or anything other than himself. He didn't feel that at ease with anyone but Adam, and even with Adam there were expectations. He'd thought Paige would have more, but her conversations about the past and her job, just the easiness of talking with her, had caused his usual defenses to melt away.

So he'd thought of her first thing this morning. And here he was, suffering.

"Oh! Towels." She pivoted to go back the way she'd come, giving him a view of her nearly naked back and mouthwatering ass.

He was already hard and gripped the edge of her counter to keep himself from following her and tasting all that gorgeous flesh.

"What time do you have to be at work?" she asked, scooping up her keys from the table by the door.

Right, work. So not enough time to swim and make love to her. Maybe they'd skip the swim. She approached with a sway that told him she knew exactly what she was doing, punishing him, no doubt. If he'd stayed that night, would she have let him back in her bed already?

Would he still want to be there? The thought kicked him in the chest. He liked the forbidden. Was he lying to himself? Was he more interested in Paige because she was holding him off? The idea had him frowning when she stopped in front of him.

"Can you hold my keys?" She let her fingertips drag down the inside of his wrist as she dropped the keychain into his palm. "I don't have a place to keep them." She spread her arms, as if he wasn't already looking.

"Sure." He cleared his throat when the one word came out in a croak, and tucked the keys in his pocket. "Your roommate and CeCe?"

She met his gaze with a knowing smile. "They'll be up in a bit so CeCe can go to nursery school."

So no wall-banging sex. No, the next time they made love, he wanted her so crazy she screamed. Wouldn't do to have an impressionable kid in the next room. Just as well. He needed to figure out what he was really doing here.

He stepped toward the door. "Shall we go?"

The pool sparkled in the early-morning sunlight. As she'd said, they had it to themselves. He hoped the water was cold enough to douse his arousal, because watching the play of muscles in her back as he walked behind her had him harder than he'd been since the last time he'd seen her.

Once they reached the edge of the pool, she tossed the towels on a nearby lounge chair and dove in without hesitation. He watched her body cut gracefully through the water before she surfaced at the other end, pushed her hair out of her face and grinned.

"Brr!" Her laugh echoed off the surrounding buildings.

"Good." He stripped off his shirt, tossed it on the lounge with their towels and followed her in.

The water was colder than hell, thank God, but when he swam up to Paige, his cock forgot the rules about cold water. He wanted to take her hand from where it rested on the side of the pool and rub it over his erection.

His willpower frayed, and his gaze was drawn to the gleam of water on her breasts, the way her nipples thrust against the knit fabric. He could almost taste them in his mouth. Had he given her breasts enough attention when they'd made love? He couldn't remember, but he wanted another chance now.

"I'll race you," she said, bracing herself against the side of the pool in readiness.

He had to drag his attention back to her face. She watched him with the clear confidence of a woman who knew what she wanted. He should be lucky he was the object of that focus.

"I'm a head taller than you, and my arms are longer," he pointed out.

"So give me a head start."

He eyed the length of the pool, not very long. "Not sure that will work."

"Just race me, to the other end and back." She gathered her legs beneath her, ready to push off.

"Fine." He had the handicap of wearing his basketball shorts instead of his swimming trunks anyway. "You say go."

"On your mark," she said, with a bounce. "Get set." Another bounce. "Go!"

His chivalrous thought to give her a head start was defeated by his competitiveness. He swam alongside her, then past her, reaching the other end of the pool before taking a breath and flipping to swim the other way. He was aware of her nearby, but unprepared for her to swim beneath him like a damn mermaid, her legs tangling with his as her body slid against him, breasts to chest, before she straightened to swim past him. He had to lift his head above water to catch his breath. Only then could he could follow, and found her waiting at the edge of the pool.

"That's cheating," he accused, standing and shoving his dripping hair back from his face.

"How, exactly?" she asked tartly.

"You distracted me."

She moved closer, and he couldn't bring himself to back away as she placed her palm over his thundering heart. "How did I distract you?"

"You know what you did," he growled, that frayed leash on his willpower snapping as he closed his hands around her bare waist and drew her in for a kiss.

She folded her arms around his neck and rubbed her breasts against his chest, bare skin and erect nipples only making him harder. He pressed her into the side of the pool, and her legs parted around his hips, opening her to him. All he had to do was push aside that little scrap of fabric, and he'd be inside her, feeling her gripping him, hot and slick.

He bumped her hips as he thrust his tongue in her mouth and her hands coursed down his back as she returned the kiss, nipping and sucking, her mouth hot and eager. He cupped her breast, resisting the urge to push the fabric away and taste her skin. She pressed into his hand for a moment before breaking the kiss and easing back as far as she could with the wall of the pool behind her.

"So you want a do-over?" she asked breathlessly through lips swollen by his kiss.

Sure, if that's what she wanted to call it. "Hell yes."

She slipped from beneath his arm and hung on the edge of the pool, as she'd done before the race.

"I'm not going to race you again," he said, understanding

dawning, disappointment blooming. "I had a different kind of exercise in mind."

She widened her eyes in mock innocence. "Here?"

"Your apartment."

"Gloria and CeCe will be up."

He swore. "How long until they leave?"

"Well, Gloria gives CeCe her breakfast and they get dressed. Gloria takes CeCe to daycare, then comes home to go back to bed."

Message received. He shifted his weight onto his heels. "So it's not happening this morning."

"Sorry."

She didn't look sorry at all. She eased closer in the water so her breath gusted against his throat. "Do you want to fuck me or make love to me?"

"What's the difference?" As soon as the words left his mouth, he knew he'd made a mistake.

Her eyes shuttered. "Until you know, it's not happening."

He went completely still when she unzipped his pocket and reached in, her hand so close to his throbbing cock, aware of just what she was doing, damn her. She drew out her keys and backed toward the ladder.

"Dinner tonight?" he managed when she climbed from the pool and picked up a towel.

"Can't. I'm babysitting tonight and tomorrow."

"I could come over."

"Nope." She tossed a towel in his direction as he emerged from the water.

"When, then?"

"I'm free Friday. Do you want to come up and change?" She indicated his dripping shorts.

See, that was how being with her short-circuited his brain.

"I didn't bring anything else." So he'd be soaking the driver's seat of his car. Hell.

"You can bring the towel back Friday. Shall we say seven?"

Before he could respond, she swayed off toward the stairs. Yeah, all that and he hadn't even gotten his exercise.

Adam called later that morning, and while Zach's first instinct was to ignore it—since he'd spent the better part of the morning fantasizing about Zach's sister—he picked up.

"So about those two girls," Adam began.

Zach frowned before he remembered Adam had promised details in retaliation for Zach backing out of their plans. "You're a liar."

"I'm not. Gorgeous, gorgeous blondes, and very flexible. I could still hook you up."

"When was the last time I needed you to get me a woman?"

"Well, there was that time..." Adam trailed off into a chuckle. "So let's go do something tonight."

Maybe that was a good idea. Go out. See other women, have a few drinks with his friend, forget he wanted to kiss every inch of his friend's sister. Once he got his mind off of her, maybe he'd start thinking straight again, and could walk away. Maybe she wasn't what he wanted after all.

"Yeah, okay. Where are we going?"

This was his life. The music and the drinks and the gorgeous women wearing the skimpy dresses and fuck-me heels and smiling to let him know they were more than willing to go home with him.

"That brunette over there is watching you." Adam leaned on the table and motioned with his drink.

Zach was aware. The woman in question had made certain he knew she wore no underwear, and that she'd recently visited a salon. His dick stirred—it was a pussy, after all—but he didn't turn back in her direction. "Yeah, I don't think so."

Adam lifted his eyebrows. "You don't think so? What exactly were you sick with this week? Nothing dick-threatening, I hope."

Zach snorted and took a sip. "No." Unless Adam found out who he'd been spending time with.

"Because usually, that level of availability works for you."

"Maybe I'm in the mood for a bit more mystery." Or at least a bit more of a challenge. He stopped his thoughts from going to Paige. She wasn't the complete cause of his discontent. But the persona he took into the clubs with him didn't fit so well anymore. He hadn't even realized he had a persona, not until he didn't have to use it with Paige.

"So you haven't had sex in, how long?"

Zach leveled a look at his friend. "I don't need you around to get laid."

Adam scoffed. "Since when?"

Zach grinned and tried to relax. He danced with a few girls to get Adam off his back, but none of them held his attention. He ignored the concern on his friend's face when Adam approached with the panty-less brunette tucked under his arm.

"Take my car." Zach offered the keys. "I'll get a cab."

Adam frowned, but took the keys and headed out.

Paige knew she was taking a chance showing up at Zach's apartment in the morning. Just because he'd been coming around didn't mean he wasn't sleeping with someone else, or heading to the sex club for a meaningless hookup. The idea made her stomach clench. She'd done meaningless sex before and didn't see the appeal, but Zach clearly had no trouble with it. It was different for men. Her brother Adam was the same, though Matt had figured out what she had—that love was the answer.

So her stop at the coffee shop for coffee and pastries to share with him had been impulsive, and maybe a mistake. She scanned the parking lot and didn't see Zach's silver sedan. Her chest squeezed. He hadn't come home last night. Though he'd run out on her, he'd spent the night somewhere else.

She shouldn't jump to conclusions. He could have gone for a run or to the gym, or he could have crashed at Adam's. But her imagination took her to worse places. She glanced down at the cup holder and sighed. Her cubicle mate Teresa would appreciate a slightly cold coffee and a turnover, she was sure.

She turned her car around and saw a flash of silver entering the parking lot. Oh, shit. She did not want Zach to see her. He'd think she was checking up on him, which she absolutely wasn't. She'd just wanted to share a cup of coffee with him before work. That she'd gotten a dose of reality was entirely her own fault. Quickly, she pulled into a parking space, shut off the car and slid down in her seat, out of sight.

Because she couldn't resist catching sight of him, she rose just enough to peer over the dashboard. She couldn't see the car, but she would be able to see him when he reached the stairs.

Only it wasn't Zach. Adam, wearing a rumpled suit and a big grin, trotted up the stairs to Zach's place.

Shit. Shit. Even worse if he saw her. He'd think she was leaving Zach's place, and that would cause all kinds of problems for him and Zach. Why on earth had she insisted on the blue Mini, which stood out among all the silver and black BMWs and Escalades in Zach's parking lot. Adam was going to spot her instantly.

Maybe if he went in, she could zip out of here. Please, Zach, invite him in. Please, Zach.

As she watched, Zach opened the door, Adam dangled the keys...and Zach saw her car. He did a double-take, and he grasped Adam's shoulder, presumably to keep him from turning around. She wished she knew what he was saying—she should be able to hear it, because he was talking loud enough, as if volume would blind Adam or something—but his words didn't carry as well as his voice. He stepped back into his apartment, waving in invitation. Paige couldn't see her brother's face, but the set of his shoulders made her think he was suspicious. Well, sure, who'd ever seen Zach act like that? But he followed his friend inside and closed the door. Paige wasted no time turning the ignition and beating it out of there.

She sent the first text before she reached her desk. I'm sorry!

She didn't have to wait long for a reply.

What were you doing here? His impatience was clear.

I brought coffee and turnovers.

Checking up on me.

No! No no no no no. I just wanted to see you.

In the morning.

When we wouldn't be tempted to do anything that might make us late for work.

Nothing for several minutes. She watched the phone's screen as if willing it to light up.

Adam didn't suspect, he texted finally.

Good.

I hate texting. Takes too long. See you tomorrow.

She waited again, thinking her phone would ring, that he would want to talk to her instead, but it didn't.

Around noon, though, she got another text.

Saw this and thought of you.

Frowning, unable to imagine what it could be, she clicked on the picture. The mermaid statue he'd snapped a photo of, complete with curly hair and a lacy bra, had her howling with laughter.

Paige was surprised to hear the doorbell ring when she was reading CeCe a story later that night. She admonished the girl to stay on the couch while she padded to the door to peek out.

Zach grinned through the peephole and showed her the pizza box he carried.

She dropped back on her heels, stunned, then panicked. She yanked the scrunchy from her hair and pivoted to look in the mirror above the entryway table. She'd washed the makeup from her face, and she looked about fifteen years old, with all that went along with being fifteen, awkward and splotchy. And she was pale. And wearing yoga pants and one of Matt's old college T-shirts.

And Zach, her lifelong crush, was here, waiting on the other side of the door with a pizza. She was just going to have to make the best of it.

She opened the door with a bright smile and hoped that wasn't a flinch she saw when his gaze traveled up and down. "Hey. I didn't expect you."

He smiled and twirled the box on his fingertips. "Thought you might be babysitting and hungry so I came by after work."

Of course. He was wearing his suit, though his tie was history, and she was in her sloppiest clothes. Not great for the confidence there.

"We ate." A couple of hours ago. "But come on in." She stepped aside in invitation. God, he smelled good. She wanted to bury her face in his neck. The night after they'd made love, she'd smelled him on her hands all day. She longed to repeat the experience.

CeCe appeared in the doorway. "Pizza!" She clapped in excitement.

She'd almost forgotten the little girl would get so excited about pizza, even after dinner. "One tiny piece," Paige agreed. That shouldn't hurt before bedtime. "With a glass of milk."

"Shall I take it in here?" Zach motioned to the living room. "The game is on, and I thought maybe we could watch it."

Paige noticed the six-pack of beer in his other hand and

wondered if he'd shown up at the wrong Clark's apartment. "Sure. Go ahead. I'll just get CeCe's milk. CeCe, help him clear off the coffee table. And promise me you will not drop your pizza on the couch."

"I promise." CeCe followed Zach into the living room like a little rat following the Pied Piper.

Briefly Paige considered running to the bathroom and slapping on some foundation and mascara, but refrained. When she entered the living room with milk, a bottle of water for herself and an armload of napkins, she saw CeCe and Zach eying each other warily across the open box of pizza, both of them sitting on the floor on opposite sides of the coffee table. The scent of the pizza filled the room and made her stomach grumble, though she'd just had a salad a couple of hours ago.

Zach chose the channel while Paige selected the smallest piece for CeCe and the next smallest for herself. Zach twisted open a bottle of beer and washed down his own large slice. He nodded toward CeCe.

"Why is she staring at me?"

"She doesn't see a lot of men."

"You have pretty eyes," CeCe blurted, and Zach grinned at Paige, who rolled her eyes.

"Thank you," Zach said. "You have pretty eyes too. And pretty hair."

CeCe looped a curl about her fingers. "My mom says it's a bitch to comb."

Zach choked on his beer.

"Can I touch your face?"

Zach looked from CeCe's outstretched hand to Paige and raised his eyebrows. She shrugged. No telling what CeCe wanted.

"Why, CeCe?" she asked the girl.

"He has hair on his face. I want to know if it's soft or scratchy."

Zach sighed, set his beer and pizza on the coffee table and lowered his face to her reach. The sight of CeCe's pudgy little hands against the masculine cheeks sent a tug of longing through Paige so strong that she had to look away.

"What's the verdict? Soft or scratchy?" Zach asked when CeCe dropped her hands to her lap, frowning.

"Kinda both."

"Come on, CeCe. Finish up your pizza and we'll finish your story, then time for bed." Because God help her, she wanted to be alone with Zach.

He lounged on the couch watching the game when she returned from tucking CeCe in. She'd had to wash the girl up after eating the snack, and brush CeCe's teeth. And yes, she'd slapped some foundation and mascara on herself before she rejoined him.

"Good game?" She plopped on the couch behind him, her voice too loud, making her wince.

Instead he passed her an opened beer over his shoulder. "It's okay. Is she asleep?"

"Probably not for a few more minutes yet." She sipped the beer and gave in to the desire to thread her fingers through his hair. "Thanks for the pizza. You made her night."

He twisted to look at her. "Only a side benefit. What about you? Did I make your night?"

"So far." She tightened her fingers in his hair.

He understood the invitation and was on the couch beside her in a flash, his long body against hers, pressing her into the cushions as he covered her mouth with his. The kiss was deep and languid, his fingers stroking her waist in time with his tongue stroking deep in her mouth, filling her with his taste.

"You smell really good," she murmured when he lowered his mouth to her throat.

"You feel really good," he returned, cupping her breast.

God. She rolled her hips against his erection, and he groaned. "We can't...get naked," she managed when he tugged her nipple. "She might need me."

"Not a hardship," he said against her throat, sliding his fingers from her navel to her cleft and stroking her through the thin knit of the yoga pants.

His name came out on a squeak, and she clutched his shoulders, wanting him to continue, knowing that it would only lead to nakedness. She closed her hand around his wrist and removed it, but rolled onto her back so that he was over her, his legs between hers, his mouth teasing as she moved against him. He shoved up her shirt and reached inside her bra to lightly pinch her tight nipple, and broke their kiss to close his lips around it, drawing it deep. He crept his fingers down her belly again, this time easing beneath the waistband of her pants, then her panties. She arched beneath him when he reached the slick folds of flesh.

She shoved at his shoulders and sat up.

"Paige," he protested when she slipped from beneath him.

She held out a hand. "Come with me."

Zach's pulse thrummed in his ears, in his chest, in his cock. Just having her under him had felt so good, and now she was going to kick him out. Reluctantly, he took her hand, resisting the urge to sweet-talk her. She tugged him to his feet, but when she led him down the hall, she passed the front door and opened another.

Her bedroom.

He felt a little light-headed as she guided him inside, pushed him into a sitting position on the corner of the queen-sized bed, and stood before him with her hands on her hips.

"You've been very patient. I think you deserve a reward."

"Come here," he said. "This is one of my favorite fantasies."

She placed her hands on his shoulders and bent to brush her mouth over his. "So I'll have to do my best." Her lips drifted down his throat to the opening of his shirt, her fingers floating lower, over the buckle of his belt, which she fumbled with a moment before loosening it. She let her knuckles brush over his erection through the fabric, and he groaned.

She knelt before him, unzipped his slacks and freed him. Her breath gusted over his hot skin, and he squeezed his eyes shut, fighting for control when she wrapped her fingers around him. But he had to see, had to watch her, that gorgeous hair spilling over his thighs as she guided the head of him to her mouth, running her tongue up the length of him, circling the rim of his cock before taking him deep, until her lips met her caressing touch.

He braced his hands on the bed behind him, curling his fingers in the blue and white comforter so he wouldn't bury them in her hair and thrust against her mouth. As aroused as he was, he wanted to feel what she'd do to him.

She pumped him slowly as her tongue stroked along his length, and she pulled with gentle suction. He ground his teeth as she moved up and down, holding back the orgasm when he wanted to lift his hips and let loose. He angled back on the bed so he could watch her face, those fantasy-inspired lips wrapped around him, the adoring expression on her face. His balls drew up, and her tongue fluttered right below the ridge of his head, then she slowed again, easing him back from the edge.

"Christ, Paige."

She released him with a smile. "It'll be good, I promise."

Of that, he had no doubt. She was amazing, applying just the right amount of pressure, varying the rhythm, Jesus, even nibbling. Where the hell had she learned how to give head?

He pushed the thought away, not wanting to imagine her between any other man's legs.

Finally he could resist no longer. He lifted one hand to curve around the back of her head, meeting her rhythm. She shifted her touch so her fingernails teased his tight balls and he lost it, no longer able to hold back, heat shooting through him, and he came with a groan in slow, hard pulses. She removed her hand to take him deeper, into her throat, licking until he dropped back to the bed, spent.

"I was a very, very good boy," he said to the ceiling.

She laughed and stretched beside him. "Yes you were."

He turned his face to her, sweeping his thumb over her swollen lower lip. God, she was a fantasy come to life. "I also have excellent manners. If someone does something nice to me, I return the favor."

"You don't have to." But she rolled on her back when he rose over her, toying with the tie of her yoga pants. "Don't take my clothes off."

"I like a challenge." He could already smell her arousal. He shifted so she parted her legs for him. He tweaked her nipple, kissed her belly where the T-shirt had ridden up, and closed his mouth over her pussy through the thin knit of the pants.

She bowed beneath him, having no qualms whatsoever to digging her fingers into his scalp, holding him to her. The sound she made, a low, guttural, needy sound was sexy as hell—and alarming, with a kid in the next room. He lifted his head to look up at her chidingly.

"You want me to gag you?"

The catch of her breath made him think she found the idea arousing, and he made a note to try it at some point in the future. Right now he wanted to drive her out of her mind. He circled his mouth above her clit and she bumped her hips against him, wanting more. Teasing her wasn't enough. He wanted to fill his mouth with the taste of her. She protested when he pulled down the front of the knit pants and panties to bare her pussy to him. He glided his tongue along the slick folds, stroking her entrance with the flat of his tongue, before flicking against her swollen clit, feeling it quiver, feeling an echoing shudder run through her body. He repeated the playful caress, and she lifted her hips, burrowing her fingers in his hair to guide him back to where she wanted him. As much as he didn't want to end this yet, he obliged, parting her for his mouth, sliding one finger inside her.

He managed to cover her mouth as she came with a cry, pumping against him, filling him with her taste and an odd sense of triumph. A glance up the length of her body showed her throat stretched, her body arched in the pleasure he gave her. Sexiest thing he'd ever seen.

He wanted to be inside her again but wanted all night to enjoy it, not stolen moments while she was babysitting.

He rose to kiss her, the taste of his come on her lips enough to make him stir already. But then she tucked her head under his chin, her fingers curling in the front of his shirt, murmured something he didn't understand, and soon, her breathing evened out in the rhythm of sleep.

Well, hell.

A pounding on the bedroom door woke Zach. For a moment, he didn't know where he was, but the cloud of curls around his face clued him in. Paige's bed. God knew what time it was.

"Aunt Paige!" cried a frantic voice, followed my more knocking. "I threw up in my bed."

Paige tensed, then scrambled from beneath his arm, leaving him to realize too late that he'd spooned against her in his sleep and held her breast.

"Sorry," she muttered. "Watch the light."

He closed his eyes too late and saw spots when she flicked on the bedside lamp. Before he recovered and looked up, she'd twisted her hair up in a scrunchy and opened the door.

"Oh, honey," he heard her say before the scent of pizza vomit wafted toward him.

He rolled to his feet, not quite awake. "What can I do?"

"Don't worry. I'm just going to bathe her and clean it up. I'll be back in a few."

She guided the crying child out of the room, and a few minutes later he heard the water running. He glanced at the clock. Not even midnight. When was the last time he'd been asleep before midnight?

He staggered into the hall, where the scent of vomit was stronger. He swallowed his own gag. CeCe said she'd thrown up in her bed. Easy enough to find the open door. He flipped on the light, and wow. Yeah, she'd thrown up. He wouldn't be eating pizza again for a while. Taking a deep breath in the hall, he strode across the room and stripped off the soiled bedding, inspecting the stuffed animals for any residual damage. Nothing too bad, nothing a sponge couldn't take care of.

Once the bedding was wadded, he carried it into the hall. The air was a bit more breathable now. He tapped on the bathroom door.

Paige opened the door, brow furrowed, hair frazzled, sleepy eyed. Gorgeous. He took a step back. "I'll take the clothes down to the laundry room. Give me her pajamas."

Her eyes widened as she looked from the pile of clothes to his face. "You didn't have to do that."

"Paige. I'm holding pukey laundry. Give me her pajamas and tell me where the laundry room is."

She ducked back in the bathroom and returned in seconds with towel-wrapped pj's. "There's a laundry room on every floor. Go right all the way to the end of the hall. You need a code. It's seventy-two, seventy-three. And you'll need quarters and the laundry detergent is under the sink." She sagged against the door. "You don't have to do this," she said again.

"I'll be back."

He located the detergent, then slipped into the hall and down to the laundry room. He entered the code, loaded the washer and dropped into one of the molded plastic chairs as the washer filled with water. What the hell was he doing here? He didn't want a connection like this, didn't want to care like this. Just because she was beautiful and gave great blowjobs and was funny and sweet—this wasn't in the plans. Maybe someday, when he was forty, tired of going out all the time, he'd find a woman like Paige and settle down, maybe even have a couple of kids of his own. He'd have the money. He wouldn't struggle as his own parents had done. His kids would go to private schools, get new cars, have college paid for so they didn't have to work so hard. And he wouldn't have to scrimp to make that happen. He wasn't there yet, and so he wasn't ready for a woman to charge into his life with her need for romance.

He scrubbed his hands over his face. Time to bail.

As soon as the laundry was done.

When he returned to the apartment, he followed the sound of quiet singing to Paige's bedroom. She was curled around CeCe on the bed, stroking her curls and crooning to her. The child's eyes drifted shut, opened again, then drifted. The sight made his gut ache in a way he couldn't define. Without changing her movements, Paige shifted her gaze to him and smiled.

"The bedding's in the dryer," he told her. "It'll probably be a while."

"Thank you," she murmured in the same singsong voice. "You helped me a lot. I would have had to leave her alone to wash, or carry her with me."

"Yeah, well, I was here. And it wasn't my first time." His youngest brother was always throwing up—on the bus, in bed, on the lunchroom table. He shuddered at the mortifying memory. "But I'm going to go."

He thought he saw disappointment flicker in her eyes before she turned her attention back to CeCe.

"Okay. Thanks again. Good night." Without taking her gaze from the girl, she angled her face as if for a kiss, but he backed out the door and bolted.

Chapter Six

Paige shouldn't have been surprised to get the call from Zach breaking their Friday date with the weak excuse of a business dinner, but the message hurt nonetheless. Worse that he left a message, instead of having the balls to speak to her and have her ask why.

Though she knew why. Last night came too close to domesticity for him. He was enough like her brother that she understood that. The two of them fed off each other when it came to the lifestyle of confirmed bachelors.

The two men had come to accept whatever the other was doing as favorable. What she didn't know was why any other choice was so distasteful to them.

She wanted to charge over to Zach's and demand he man up, that he at the very least admit the truth about why he broke the date. But that would only make him defensive. So she'd wait, and see if his guilt—or better, his desire for her—brought him around.

She never thought she'd have enough patience, especially as the weekend dragged. She agreed to go out with her friend Teresa and half-expected to see Zach at one of the clubs they hit

Saturday night. She danced with a number of guys, and imagined Zach walking in and having a fit of jealousy, maybe storming over and laying a kiss on her, proclaiming his love in front of everyone. But of course that didn't happen, and despite the best efforts of several of her dance partners, she went home alone.

She was awakened by a phone call Sunday morning. Groggy from her late night, and maybe a little too much to drink, she didn't look at the caller ID before answering it.

"I tried to call you last night but there was no answer," Zach said petulantly.

She sat up and tucked her arms around her knees. Of course he'd call now, when she wasn't her best. "I went out," she said.

"And didn't take your phone?"

She drew the phone away to look at the display, but didn't see any missed calls noted. "I must have been in a place with bad reception. I don't see your call."

"I was just wondering how CeCe was feeling," he said, pique still in his tone.

His reason softened her a little. Not that it took much. She was a sucker when it came to Zach Purser. "Better. We found out that she snuck out after you and I—came in here, and she ate two more pieces of pizza. Made herself sick. Thanks again for doing the laundry."

He grunted. "Do you want to go to dinner tonight? I can get us reservations at a nice restaurant downtown."

"Can get or did get?" she asked.

"Would that make a difference?"

It would make her think he was maybe too sure of her. But she wasn't one to play hard to get. "Not really."

"So do you want to go, or did you meet someone last night?"

She took a deep breath and called herself a fool, but said, "I would like to go."

"I'll pick you up at eight." But instead of staying on the line to talk, he disconnected.

Well. At least she had the day to pick out a gorgeous new dress.

Two days without seeing Paige was interminable. Zach stopped for flowers on the way to her apartment, and he couldn't remember the last time he brought a woman flowers. Couldn't remember the last time he wanted to see someone this bad. Couldn't remember the last time he wanted someone this bad. No other woman would satisfy him. He hadn't even been tempted.

Paige opened the door wearing a pretty red halter dress with a flowing skirt, her hair pinned away from her face but tumbling down her back. And damn it, he couldn't help himself. He curved his hand around her waist and lowered his mouth to hers, not caring that he messed up her lipstick, just wanting the taste of her.

She looked up at him with a sigh of appreciation and smiled with her whole face, her hands on his arms. He presented the Gerber daisies to her with a flourish and a bow. Her eyes brightened in delight.

She introduced him to her roommate Gloria as she turned to put the flowers in water, and he was too aware of Gloria's disapproval as she watched him.

"What?" he asked.

"Don't you raise her expectations and then destroy them," Gloria warned. "I know men like you."

His shoulders stiffened at the broad brushstroke with which he'd been painted, his delight in seeing Paige's excitement dissipating. "I have no intention of hurting her."

"You may not, but it's going to happen anyway. You don't stick around, do you? And Paige wants someone who'll stick around. She wants you to be that someone."

His stomach knotted at the truth of the words. Paige deserved so much better than him. But he couldn't walk away yet. He didn't have the willpower.

She returned and looped her arm through his, facing Gloria. "I can take care of myself, Glo, and you know it."

Gloria made a sound that told him she knew of no such thing. Paige broke away from Zach and crossed the room to kiss her friend on the cheek.

"I'll be fine. I know what I'm doing."

"Does everyone feel like they have to protect you from yourself?" Zach asked as they walked down to his car.

"Everyone but you," she replied brightly.

"That's because I'm the big bad wolf and you're Little Red Riding Hood." He opened the passenger door, and when she climbed in, he gave her skirt a playful flip.

He couldn't keep his gaze off her. He'd chosen an intimate place for dinner, and they were tucked in a booth near the dance floor, where he had every intention of getting his hands on her.

"Are you going to stare at my cleavage all night?"

"I'm hoping to rescue any bits of dip that land there."

"I've had these boobs for years. I know how to eat with them."

He leaned on the table. "Just a little drop. Give me a thrill."

She only smiled and returned the wonton to the bowl. He grinned in return and signaled for another drink when a man slid into an empty chair at the table. Zach straightened, not recognizing the newcomer at first. He sat back, some of the pleasure of the evening leaching from him.

"Brandon. Good to see you." His voice conveyed a different message entirely. He didn't want this man anywhere near Paige. She was different, and while he wasn't ashamed of the things he'd done, he didn't want to imagine how she would see his past.

Brandon looked appreciatively at Paige. "Who is this?"

"Paige, this is Brandon. He clearly doesn't pick up on social cues." He turned to his, well, friend was not the right word. "We're on a date."

"A real date?" Brandon's brows lifted, and his even white teeth flashed.

"Yes, a real date. Beat it."

"Oh, come on, Zach. She's a knockout. You don't want to share?"

"Time to go." Zach pushed his chair back. He couldn't look at Paige, didn't want to see her reaction.

Brandon had shifted as Zach moved his chair, but didn't rise. "Are you sure she's not willing?"

"I'm not willing." He didn't want anyone else. Being around Paige had seen to that. Zach rose and reached a hand to her. From the corner of his eye, he saw her eyes were wide as she looked from one to the other. "We're going to dance. Don't be here when we return."

He turned Paige into his arms on the dance floor and sensed her impatience. He didn't have long to wait before she asked.

"Did he want a—three-way?"

"Yes."

"With—me?"

His gut clenched. Surely she wouldn't consider such a thing. "Yeah."

"Have you—before? Of course you have, or he wouldn't have mentioned it. How does that work?"

He hadn't expected the curiosity, only judgment. "The way you might imagine." He hoped she'd hear in his voice that he didn't want to talk about it.

"I thought a guy's fantasy was two girls. Have you done that too?" She angled her head, studying his face.

He eased back from her a bit. "Paige."

"I guess, with your looks, it makes sense."

Crap. He could hear the doubt in her voice. "I don't do that anymore."

"When was the last time?"

"Way before I saw you at the engagement party."

"How way before?"

"Last winter. An ex-girlfriend, her new boyfriend."

"I guess I can't imagine how you'd even approach something like that."

"Paige." He shifted her in his arms, finally looking into her eyes. "I don't want to talk about it, don't want him to spoil our evening, all right?"

"Okay." She cupped his shoulder and moved a little closer, but he could feel tension in her, could practically hear the wheels in her head turning as she imagined it. He didn't want her thinking about it but didn't know how to make her stop. He wasn't used to being uncomfortable in his own skin, not with her.

Until tonight, he hadn't realized his past might be just that. Those experiences no longer held the same appeal.

Maybe they both needed time to think this over. "You want to go? We could try this again tomorrow."

"No. No, I don't want to go. I'm good." She edged in a bit more and smiled up at him, more of a Paige smile, just a hint of doubt remaining. "No Adam to punch you in the face this time."

"And I actually like this dress better." He forced a smile, then relaxed into it when he saw the affection in her eyes. Pushing his discomfort to the side, he let his thumb brush the bare skin at the small of her back, and she eased closer, her fingers toying with his hair. He angled his head so that her breath brushed over his lips, just the hint of a kiss, a tease, that made him hard, made his blood sizzle. He wanted to drag her to his apartment and get her naked. At the same time, he wanted to dance with her all night and savor every moment in her arms. He looked into her eyes and saw heat there, and decided to build the anticipation, and pray that no one else interrupted them.

He didn't even hear the music anymore, didn't know if it was fast or slow, just moved with Paige at the same pace, her breasts—braless beneath the halter dress—against his chest, the skirt swaying about his legs, her hand warm on his skin. He feathered a kiss across her cheek, another across her temple, and felt her breath hitch.

"I'm ready to go," she said, her lips brushing his ear, making his erection strain.

He wasn't, but couldn't resist a kiss to the shell of her ear. "We didn't eat yet."

Her fingers tightened on the back of his neck in reflex. "I'm not hungry." Her voice was breathy, almost panicked.

His self-control frayed. This was what he'd wanted for days, and just when he'd decided to drag it out, she'd gotten desperate. God forbid he deny a lady's request. He turned her so she walked in front of him, hiding his hard-on as they made their way back to the table. He motioned for the check, paid with cash, adding a generous tip, and led Paige to the car.

Paige's pulse tripped double-time on the silent ride. She couldn't think of a single thing to say. All she could think of was the way he'd looked at her, the way he'd held her on the dance floor, the way he'd teased her with those almost-kisses. Her blood hummed through her veins, drowning out every thought of coherent conversation, blinding her to the image she'd formed in her head of him sharing a woman with another man.

He didn't speak either, just pulled into his apartment complex. He parked, sat behind the wheel for a bit—he'd better not be talking himself out of this—then pulled the keys from the ignition and walked around to open her door. She put her hand in his, wanting to squeeze—seeking reassurance or giving it, she wasn't sure. But she was aiming for sophisticated here. She let him lead her to the second-floor apartment, and watched as he unlocked the door.

She had imagined his apartment as many things, from the Dudley-Moore-like bachelor pad with everything designed to seduce, to a leather-and-black elegance. She was unprepared for the comfort of the place, the plush rust-colored leather couch, angled toward the pine entertainment set with the flat-screen TV, the granite-topped pass-through bar with a cast-iron wine rack and neat stack of newspapers. A pair of athletic shoes sat on the floor at the end of the couch. So—unpretentious. She got the feeling he always wore a mask, tried to be someone he wasn't. But here at home, here with her...

He turned her into his arms and curved his hand under her jaw, lifted her face for his kiss.

Again, not what she expected, soft, gentle, reverent as his lips moved over hers, fit over hers. His fingers tangled in the soft hair at the back of her neck. She sighed and leaned into him, her palms pressed against his chest, trapped between them. He was every fantasy come true as he explored her mouth, stroked her skin. His touch trailed down her bare shoulder, her arm, before he closed his hands over her shoulder and broke the kiss. Without a word he turned her away and drew her back against his chest. She gasped when he traced the line of her shoulder with his lips.

"Wanted to do that all night," he said against her skin. "You take my breath away."

She tried not to think that he probably said that to any number of women, only gripped the bar in front of her as his lips coasted down her spine, tingles following his touch. Her skin anticipated it, until there was nothing but his mouth and hands. He turned her again and rose at the same time to claim her mouth. She wound her arms around his neck just to stay upright and opened for his kiss.

She could taste her skin on his lips and moved against his erection until he growled a warning. She thought about growling back. After all, he wasn't even touching her, only braced his arms on the bar behind her. She was the one clinging to him, her touch restless on his chest, his shoulders, seeking the warmth of his skin, wanting to feel his naked flesh against hers. Impatient with his pace, she slid her fingers between them and worked loose the top few buttons of his shirt. She dipped her fingers inside to stroke his chest hair. God, she loved his chest hair. She wanted to be greedy and rip his shirt open, but remembered how much he spent on clothes. Pretty sure he wouldn't appreciate that. So she unbuttoned a few more, aching to feel the rasp of his hair against her nipples, which he was completely ignoring as he kissed her.

He shifted his attention to her jaw, then the sensitive skin below her ear, his stubble rasping. Her nipples were so hard they hurt, and she shifted her weight on her heels to ease the ache between her legs. Why was he torturing her?

He dragged his lips forward to tease her throat, then her collarbone. She let her head fall back as he kissed his way along the bodice of her dress, teasing her with his proximity to her nipples, still not touching her. She pushed her hips against him, but he only huffed a chuckle against her skin. She hooked her ankle around his, opening herself to him, and pushed again. This time the sound he made was almost one of pain, like he needed to be inside her as badly as she needed him.

"Touch me, Zach. Please."

"I'm touching you," he said, his mouth grazing the inside of her right breast.

"Hands. Everywhere. God, you're making me crazy."

"Payback for the last two weeks." This was said against the side of her throat.

"It hasn't been two weeks." She fisted her fingers in the front of his shirt so she didn't grab his wrists and drag his hands to her breasts.

"Feels like two years," he said against her ear.

"I'm going to come as soon as you touch me."

"I have no problem with that."

Of course not. Because she already knew one orgasm wouldn't be enough tonight.

He straightened and covered her mouth with his and finally —finally cupped her jaw. She shifted to rub against his touch, savoring the warmth of his skin before she angled her head, encouraging him to explore further.

After long moments—God, he was a good kisser—his fingertips drifted down her throat to rest on the strap of fabric that looped around her neck. She held her breath in anticipation, but instead of cupping her breast, he found the fastener beneath her hair. With a deft move, he unhooked it, and the bodice drooped, pinned between their bodies. He made no move to free it, instead finding the zipper at the small of her back with no hesitation. Of course he would have noticed how to get her out of her clothes. He'd probably been planning this move all night. Only then did he put enough space between them so that the dress fell to the floor. He gave her that heart-stopping grin and lifted her out of the puddle of fabric, one arm around her naked waist, one behind her knees.

Her heart hammered—no lover had carried her to bed before. But Zach swept her into his arms as if she weighed no more than the dress she left behind. With one hand resting below her breast, he carried her down the hall to his dimly lit bedroom and lowered her to the soft cotton comforter. He leaned over her, still completely dressed, grin fading just a bit as lust took over. She shoved at his jacket until he helped her peel it off, along with his shirt, and she arched her back to rub her aching nipples against his chest.

He allowed that for only a moment before he shifted away, bending his head to her throat, following the line to her collarbone, to the hollow at the base of her throat. His breathing was ragged as he dropped kisses down her breast.

"I didn't pay these enough attention last time. You have gorgeous breasts, Paige."

She fisted her fingers in the comforter to resist the desire to drag his head to her flesh. Finally, finally, he parted his lips over her tight nipple and sucked deep.

Wetness flooded her pussy at the sensation she'd longed for, as his tongue curled, his mouth pulled, his teeth nipped.

"Touch me. God, Zach, I'm so close."

She thought he would deny her, because he turned his head to her other breast and gave it gentler attention, his tongue moving in swirls and licks that almost distracted her from noticing his fingertips gliding down her stomach to slip under the elastic of her lace panties. She whimpered and lifted her hips toward his touch. He stroked her curls, and with one finger, he parted her, gliding over her slick flesh, the petals, the swollen bud. When she rolled her hips up, he withdrew his hand and raised his head, touching his fingers to his lips.

Tasting her. She couldn't stop the groan at the eroticism of the gesture. Her own desire overwhelmed her, and she shoved at his shoulders until he took her meaning and turned onto his back. She straddled him, her fingers fumbling for the snap of his slacks, reaching inside to close around his erection as she nuzzled his nipple, savoring the brush of his chest hair against her cheek.

She released him only long enough to drag his slacks over his muscular thighs, moving down his body until the cap of his penis tapped her cheek. She gave it a promising kiss and continued farther, helping him get naked, then moved back up to cup his cock in both hands, her gaze on his face, feeling the catch of his breath as he watched her. She rose on her knees and lifted his erection so he'd have a good view as she opened her mouth over the head of him, savoring the musky taste, sliding her tongue around the ridge of flesh, lingering on the sensitive underside that had his whole body tensing. The tendons in his throat tightened as she glided her lips down his length, her tongue sliding along the pulsing veins, her fingers slipping between his thighs to toy with his balls, her thumb rubbing rhythmically over the seam of flesh separating them.

His cockhead bumped against the back of her throat, and she hesitated before opening her throat, closing her lips around the root of his shaft. She slid her mouth up to kiss the head of him.

He curved his hand around the back of her head. "Your mouth—Christ, Paige." He lifted his hips, pushing deeper, stretching her lips, her throat, before pushing her away, his erection sliding free.

In one smooth movement he sat up and took her mouth, the kiss deep and carnal, his tongue thrusting, rubbing along hers as he held her. Finally he released her head and cupped her hips, drawing her forward onto his lap so that the hair of his thighs rasped the insides of hers, his cock, hard and hot and heavy, rested against the top of her sex. She needed him inside her, now.

"Condom. Hurry," she demanded, her lips feeling ungainly after being stretched around his shaft.

He twisted, careful not to dislodge her, and opened the nightstand drawer. He snagged one, opened it and rolled it on. He'd barely secured it before she lifted herself over him, taking him deep in a slow slide. He watched her—not where their bodies joined, but her face, his hands resting lightly on her hips as she rose, savoring the caress of his cock along every nerve in her channel. She placed her palms on his chest and felt him holding his breath as she took him inside, squeezing her muscles along his length, watching his nostrils flare. She angled her hips forward with each thrust, letting the hair of his groin tickle her swollen clit, wanting his touch, but wanting to savor every stroke of his body, the rhythm she'd been aching for.

He leaned forward to kiss her, his teeth scraping her chin, her throat, his stubbled chin nuzzling the tops of her breasts.

"Beautiful," he said against her skin. "Gorgeous. Jesus, Paige."

He flexed his hips into hers, deepening the thrusts, making her gasp. She folded her arms around his shoulders and held on as he drove into her, his fingers gripping her hips, spreading her legs wider so her pussy was completely open to him. Each thrust caressed her clit, sending heat shooting through her blood, winding her up until she couldn't breathe. Then, his head tilted back so he could watch her, Zach brushed his thumb over the aching bud.

Despite her earlier claims that she'd go off the minute he touched her, the suddenness of the orgasm shocked her. That little caress sent fire spiraling through her blood as her muscles gripped along his thrusting shaft, trying to grasp every sensation, trying to draw out the orgasm.

But there was no time to catch her breath before he tilted her onto her back, spreading her legs wider, and pounded into her, balls-deep. She stroked his damp temple, watching the intensity in his features soften to pleasure before he dropped his forehead to hers, buried deep inside so she could feel the pulsing of his cock as he came.

"Give me a few minutes," he managed at last, rising on shaking arms and withdrawing from her with a reluctance her own body echoed. "And we'll go again. I can't get enough of you."

Paige drew in a breath as he rolled off the bed and headed into the bathroom to discard the condom. She couldn't ruin tonight by wondering what that meant—if he was talking about sex tonight or if he had something more lasting in mind.

No, she wouldn't do that to herself. She'd enjoy the time they had, and she'd see what the morning would bring.

Paige blinked against the sunlight that streamed through the window. She lifted her head from the pillow and looked around. Zach's bedroom. No Zach. She stretched on the very soft, no-doubt-expensive white sheets and sat up to look around.

The room was impeccably neat—even her dress hung on the hook on the closet door. Curiosity getting the better of her, she slipped out of bed and peeked into the closet. Suits were lined together on one side, with dress shirts beside them, and on the other side, jeans and more casual clothes. Did most men have this many clothes? She was certain most weren't this neat. She selected a denim shirt from a hanger—Ralph Lauren, of course —and slipped it on before stepping into an equally neat bathroom lined with pricey shaving products. After she attended to business, she took a deep breath and padded into the living room.

Zach sat at the breakfast bar with a bowl of cereal in front of him. He was dressed for work, minus his jacket and tie, and completely uncomfortable. Right away, she knew. He was shutting her out again.

He pushed to his feet but didn't look at her. "Want some cereal? I'm not much of a breakfast person, so that's all I have on hand."

She took a deep breath to ease her shaking and put on what she hoped was a cheerful smile. Maybe if they got out of here, he'd relax, since he clearly didn't want her in his space. "I'm already going to be late for work. Why don't we go out for breakfast?"

His answering smile was more of a grimace. "I'm not much of a go-out-for-breakfast person either. And all you have is your red dress."

She shrugged, though her shoulders were so tight she thought they'd snap. "We could go by my apartment so I could change." But she already knew it wouldn't happen, even as he said her name on a sigh. She straightened. Pride wouldn't allow her to release the tears that burned the backs of her eyes. He'd had her so convinced he wanted her, beyond the bedroom. Fool her once, and all that. "Right. Well, I'll get dressed and you can call me a cab."

"I'll take you home."

She didn't think she could hold on to her composure that long. "No need." She'd hoped for a breezier tone, but heard the strain in it. She turned toward the bedroom, unable to look at him.

"Paige. I just don't—no one ever spends the night."

Temper took over and she whirled on him. "You could have easily woken me and taken me home. Then I wouldn't be late."

His jaw tightened like he wanted to say something but didn't, and he stared at a spot over her shoulder. That only made her angrier. She strode across the room toward him. Her inner five-year-old wanted to shove him in the chest with both hands.

"You think you want your sacred space." She spread her hands to encompass the apartment. She hoped he didn't see how she was shaking. "This is what's important to you. But you're lonely, trying to fill something that's missing, or you wouldn't go out every night. You want everything so orderly so you can be in control, and I'm messing that up. But you're the one who came to my apartment, Zach Purser. You came to me. You think you're Mr. Aloof-and-Cool but you really don't like to be alone. You came to spend time with me twice. Twice, Zach. I didn't worm my way in here. You came to me."

His lips pressed in a thin line but he said nothing, just kept his eyes lowered. She wanted to snap her fingers in front of his face, anything to get a response.

Stepping back, she yanked his shirt over her head, hearing the rip of fabric echo in the silent room. A flicker of distress darkened his expression as she dropped the shirt in a heap in the middle of the floor and marched naked back into the bedroom for her dress. She grabbed it off the hook and dropped it over her head, then looked around the immaculate room. She wanted to knock things off the dresser, tear garments from hangers, but she calmed herself. She'd known what she was getting into here. She knew who he was. That she wanted him to be someone else was her own fault.

He stood by the front door when she strode out of the bedroom.

"Let me take you home," he offered in a maddeningly calm voice. "I can even take you to work if you'd like."

God. Work. She wasn't going to be able to hold herself together at work. She'd have to call in, but damned if she'd let him know that.

"I can take care of myself, Zach." She positioned herself in front of him so that he had no choice but to look into her eyes. "I'm all grown up now. I'll wait for the cab downstairs, if you'll be so kind as to call. I'm sure you have their number on speed-dial."

He stepped back and lifted the phone. She didn't wait to see if she was right about speed-dial. That would have just been too much. Instead, she swung open the door with as much aplomb as she could gather and marched down the stairs.

She didn't let the tears come until she was home in her room.

Chapter Seven

Matt and J.R. had decided they didn't want separate bachelor parties, but one big party the week before the wedding to celebrate the, well, the celebration. Which meant Paige would see Zach this weekend, like it or not. He'd called—she'd give him that—but she'd let the three attempts go to voice mail. The first time, he hadn't left a message. The other two were stilted apologies, but no invitation to meet face to face. Maybe he was scared she'd go to Adam and tell him to kick Zach's ass.

No, if anyone was going to kick it, she was. She might get her chance at this party.

Now she just needed a shield. So she bought a new eat-your-heart-out dress and shoes way beyond her budget. And she asked Matt to fix her up with one of his friends from work. She loathed the idea of a blind date, but she trusted her brother, and she needed something to occupy her thoughts, which would otherwise be filled with seeing Zach.

She didn't tell Matt that, of course.

"I know just the guy," Matt told her over the phone. "Handsome, well-dressed, successful."

"So why doesn't he already have a date?"

"He may be a little gay. He just doesn't know it yet."

That surprised a laugh from her. Maybe she wouldn't be as occupied as she hoped.

"Should I tell him to pick you up?"

"No, if things don't work out I don't want to have to worry about getting home. I'll just meet him there."

Matt and J.R. had rented an upscale restaurant downtown for the occasion. Paige arrived about halfway through the cocktail hour, wishing she hadn't fallen quite so in love with shoes that hurt after walking three blocks from the only parking space she'd been able to find. She smoothed her skirt and scanned the place for Zach—she'd looked for his car on the way here too—but didn't see him. She ordered a martini and accepted it just as Matt called her name.

Her brother looked radiantly happy as he hugged her, then pulled her forward, toward the row of windows overlooking the city.

"Your date's here."

Nerves tickled her stomach, and she inspected the tables, looking for a man alone. She found one, his back to her, thick brown hair impeccably combed, expensive suit neatly pressed, and familiarity kicked those nerves into high gear. She dug in her heels, pulling her arm free from Matt's.

"You've got to be kidding me."

Her brother turned with a knowing smile. "He asked, Paige."

"He asked you to let me make a scene at your party?"

Matt's expression was indulgent. "He asked me to help him make it up to you. He said you weren't answering his calls."

"He wasn't exactly Mr. Persistent."

"Maybe he has something in mind."

Zach turned, and Paige realized he'd been watching her

reflection in the glass. All her shields were useless as she looked into his eyes. He offered her that tilted smile that made her stomach flutter, and rose.

"Can we talk? Outside?" He nodded toward a door leading to a balcony overlooking the river.

Better than in here. She jerked her head in response and stepped toward him, aware of Matt watching. She resisted the urge to glare at him—she'd save that for later.

Zach held the door for her. She should have held her breath, because the scent of him—his expensive shaving cream and soap —hit her right in the solar plexus. She wanted to turn into his arms with no hesitation. Instead she gathered her pride and marched past him, head held high.

The breeze off the river was cool, and Paige fought a shiver, instead stoking a fire of anger as she turned to him.

"I'm sorry," he said, leaning against the iron rail.

"For what, exactly?" She cocked her hip and wished these damned shoes in the river.

He edged toward her but kept his arms folded over his chest. "You were right," he said in a tone she hadn't heard before, part charming and part—something she couldn't name. "I guard my privacy—I have since I got my own place. And I guard it so well I don't even know how to share it with someone I want there."

She mirrored his posture, but countered the defensiveness with honesty. "You didn't want me there. That was clear."

"I didn't know what to do with you when you were there," he said. "Other than the obvious."

The wind whipped her hair into her face, and she shoved it back with an impatient hand. "I wouldn't have minded another round of the obvious. I wouldn't have minded if we spent all day in bed." And she'd fantasized about that often enough. "But I felt so unwelcome, like an intruder, and it felt unfair because you brought me there. You invited me. I felt like—

another conquest. Maybe I am." She gave up on the shield of her folded arms and tossed her hands up. Just looking at him made her heart ache. Knowing she'd asked for too much made her feel foolish. "Maybe once you got me back in bed, you felt like you won. And maybe it's my fault for thinking it was more."

His brow furrowed in a pained expression. "You knew from the beginning that I'm not good at this."

Her stomach dropped. She hadn't even realized until now that she'd hoped his apology would lead to the next step in their relationship. She'd been prepared to take the step, though her guard would be higher. He'd fooled her twice. She wouldn't fall for it a third time. But now he was saying it was over. She couldn't quite catch her breath.

"I don't know how to be part of a couple. I haven't let myself try in a long time. I haven't wanted to try."

"Why are you doing this here?" she managed past the lump in her throat, gesturing toward the party on the other side of the door.

"I need you to understand. I want them to understand. I wanted them to know what you mean to me." He inclined his head to where Matt and her parents were watching them through the window. He took her hands, both of them in both of his, and lifted them to his chest. "I suck at this. I don't know what to do, and I'm going to stumble and screw up and hurt you when I don't do what you expect. But I don't want you to run away. I want you to teach me, and show me what makes you happy and what a boyfriend is supposed to do."

Confusion clouded her head. "What?"

He angled his head and gave her that breathtaking smile, smoothing her hair back from her face. "I'm saying I want to be with you. I want to try to be a proper boyfriend, and I'm going to fuck up and you're going to have to smack me upside the head until I get it right. But I want to get it right. Do you think you can give me another chance?"

His face blurred and danced before her, but suddenly it didn't matter because she was nodding and his hands were on her face and he was kissing her, his taste familiar and lovely and...

"What. The. Hell?"

Paige broke the kiss and pivoted to see Adam standing in the door, lip curled, shoulders squared.

"What did I tell you about touching my sister?" Adam snarled, advancing.

"It's not like that." Zach grasped her arm and drew her behind him.

Paige resisted, remembering the last time Adam had caught Zach touching her, the bruise on Zach's face.

"You come here, invited as part of the family, and you put your hands on her?"

"Stop it, Adam," she demanded, restraining herself from stomping her foot in frustration at all the testosterone flying around. "We've been seeing each other for a while."

"Because he's trying to get you into bed."

"He didn't have to try hard." She could have bitten off her tongue when she saw the colors Adam's face turned before he lunged forward.

Zach threw a hand out to stop him, then blew out a breath when Adam hesitated. "It's not like that. She's my g-girlfriend."

Paige pivoted at his stutter, like the word was foreign to him, like he'd never said it before.

"Your what?" Adam and Paige asked at the same time, Adam's tone suspicious, Paige's breathless.

"My girlfriend." The word was more definite now. He turned to Paige, his back to Adam, but he didn't seem to care. He took her hands in his. "Mine."

Nothing was in focus but his face, the uncertain furrow of his brow, the intensity of his gaze. She ducked her head against his chest, her arms around him. He drew her close and sighed in relief as he buried his face in her hair.

Paige was close enough to feel the tap on his shoulder.

Zach lifted his head and turned toward Adam, and his best friend punched him in the face.

Epilogue

The bruise had faded by Matt and J.R.'s wedding. Zach looked down at his hand folded around Paige's on the table at the reception. He hadn't been able to keep his eyes off her at the ceremony, and now he couldn't stop touching her. Okay, that had happened before, but the hand-holding thing, that was something he'd never really enjoyed.

Except with Paige.

And he loved watching her. She'd enjoyed every aspect of her brother's commitment ceremony, teared up during it, hell, sobbed until her breath came in hitches and her nose was red. So fucking adorable. Now her smile was brilliant as she watched her brother and his life partner dance to the old Dean Martin song. Zach had every intention to get her on the dance floor too, though he'd have to mind his manners since her parents were here.

The past week had been astonishing. Paige stayed over on nights when she wasn't babysitting CeCe, had a drawer in his room, space in his closet. On nights she didn't stay over, he went to her apartment, just to be with her, and maybe make out a little. But even when he went home horny as hell, he was happy.

She had forged a peace between him and Adam, though Adam watched them warily. He and Adam were more cautious around each other now, but civil. Zach wondered if they could be as close, if Adam would eventually understand that Zach was falling in love with Paige.

Paige turned, her smile expectant.

"What'd I miss?" he asked, tucking a curl behind her ear.

"They invited us to dance. Where were you?"

He shook his head, unwilling to reveal the sappy nature of his thoughts. "Let's dance then."

"Be good," she warned, leading the way to the dance floor.

"Around you? Impossible."

Especially when she wound her arms around his neck and pressed her breasts against his chest, let her champagne-scented breath wash over his lips. Unable to resist, he dipped his head and kissed her, gently. He lifted his head and saw the glow in her eyes that reflected everything he was feeling. He smoothed her hair away from her throat. She smiled and looked toward where her brother danced with his partner. She rested her head on Zach's shoulder.

"They deserve every minute of this."

"Makes it worth everything they went through," he agreed. The pure joy radiating from the men made him want things he'd never wanted. Never thought he'd wanted.

He stepped back and took her hand.

"What are you doing?" she asked as he led her from the dance floor, almost skipping to keep up with him. When she saw he led her toward the French doors to the patio, her eyes widened. "We are not making out at my brother's wedding."

"Be quiet," he said, and opened the door onto the patio. He glanced around—he wasn't the only one with this idea. Well, not this idea. But the idea to come out on the patio. He'd hoped for privacy, but—maybe there, the lower patio overlooking the fountain. That might be perfect.

"Where are we going?"

He didn't answer, just started down the steps, her hand firm in his. He stopped near the fountain, which was busier than the patio. Looked like no one wanted to dance. Didn't matter. He was going to do this now, even if he had to go back inside on the dance floor. But he didn't want to take anything away from Matt and J.R.

He motioned for Paige to sit on the wide concrete edge of the fountain. He sat beside her with his knees angled toward her and took her hands in his. "Paige, you know more about me than any woman I've ever gone out with."

She tilted her head, her pretty forehead creasing. "Probably more than I want to know." She craned her neck to look over the rail. "Does this mean now you have to kill me?"

He huffed out a short laugh. "More than you want to know." He glanced down at the fountain. He knew how to charm women, so why weren't these words coming?

He curved his hand over her cheek and looked into her suddenly shiny eyes. "I love you, Paige. I've never said that to a woman before, ever. But I love you."

Her lips moved but no words came out at first. "You're just... Matt's wedding. You're thinking—"

"I'm thinking that I'm in love with you, Paige. You make me happy. Just thinking about you makes me happy. I've never been unhappy with my life, but since you've been in it, you made me see what I was missing."

She was crying full-out now, and panic blossomed in his chest. He didn't know how to stop her tears, so he tried to stroke them away with his fingertips.

"I've wanted to hear you say that since I was fourteen years old." She leaned in to kiss him, her mouth tight with emotion, and he folded his arms around her.

"Purser! What the hell are you doing to my sister?" Adam shouted from the top of the stairs.

Zach reacted slower than Paige, who was on her feet and turning before Zach even let her go. He stood to face his friend.

"You made her cry?" Adam's voice was incredulous as he hurried down the steps.

Paige slapped her hands on Adam's chest. "That is no way to talk to the man who just told me he loves me."

Adam's expression was almost identical to his sister's wide-eyed stare as he looked from one to the other.

Zach stepped between Paige and her brother, chin raised in challenge. "Going to hit me again?"

"You're in love? With my sister?"

Zach braced himself for the blow. "Yes."

A grin split Adam's face and when the blow came, it was a clap on the shoulder. "Welcome to the family. And if you hurt my sister, I'll kill you."

Zach looked from Adam to Paige, and a grin spread across his face as he looked into the eyes of the woman he loved. "I won't give you the chance."

About the Author

Emma Jay has been writing longer than she'd care to admit, using her endless string of celebrity crushes as inspiration for her heroes. Emma, married 35 years (wed at the age of 8, of course) believes writing romance is like falling in love, over and over again. Creating characters and love stories is an addiction she has no intention of breaking.

Also by Emma Jay

Historicals

Eye of the Beholder

Wild Wild Widow

In the Marshal's Arms

Stealing the Marshal's Heart

Contemporaries

It Happened One Night series

One Crazy Night

One Rockin' Night

One Steamy Night

One Sizzling Night

One Wanton Night

One Smokin' Night

Taming the Cowboy series

At the Cowboy's Mercy

The Cowboy's Saving Grace

Faith in the Cowboy

Bridesmaids in Paradise series

Her Perfect Getaway

Her Island Fantasy

Her Moonlit Gamble

Blackwolf Hot Shot series

All on the Line

Crossing the Line

Standing on the Line

Standalones

Riding Out the Storm

Two Step Temptation

Show Off

Off Limits

Lessons for Teacher

Two Nights on the Island

Hot and Bothered

9 798223 969198